She'd never felt so needy and vulnerable.

He must have sensed it, because he pulled her into his arms, wrapping her tight against his chest. "I'm walking through this with you, Lexi," he spoke into her hair. "No matter what happens, no matter how long it takes, I'll be right beside you. And so will God."

"Thank you." She closed her eyes and rested her head against his shoulder. His words gave her the courage she needed to get through this. They stood together in her grandparents' front yard for several minutes. She may have stayed longer, if he'd let her. He kissed the top of her head and released his hold, grabbing her hand and pulling her forward. Just before opening the front door, he paused and turned toward her, placing a hand on each side of her face. Their gazes magnetized, drawing them ever closer.

Lexi's heart beat out its own song against her ribs. She anticipated his lips meeting her own. Never had she wanted a man's kiss more.

He stopped short, resting his forehead against hers. "God loves you, Lexi. Get the idea out of your head that He's trying to punish you through this. The world is full of mean and evil people who affect innocent people's lives."

"I'm not so innocent, Cody."

JERI ODELL is a native of Tucson, Arizona. She has been married over thirty-five years and has three wonderful adult children and one precious grandbaby. Jeri holds family dear to her heart, second only to God. This is Jeri's seventh novel for Heartsong. She has also written seven novellas, a nonfiction book, and articles on family issues for several Christian publications. She thanks God for the privilege of writing for Him. When not writing or reading, she is busy in her church and community. If you'd like, you can e-mail her at jeri@jeriodell.com.

Books by Jeri Odell

HEARTSONG PRESENTS
HP413—Remnant of Victory
HP467—Hidden Treasures
HP525—Game of Pretend
HP595—Surrendered Heart
HP781—Always Yesterday
HP805—Only Today

Until Tomorrow

Jeri Odell

Heartsong Presents

To my Lord and Savior Jesus Christ. Thank You for getting me through this book.

A note from the Author:
I love to hear from my readers! You may correspond with me by writing:

> **Jeri Odell**
> **Author Relations**
> **PO Box 721**
> **Uhrichsville, OH 44683**

ISBN 978-1-60260-188-8

UNTIL TOMORROW

Our mission is to publish and distribute inspirational products offering exceptional value and biblical encouragement to the masses.

PRINTED IN THE U.S.A.

one

"I'm sorry, Alexandria, but unless you're willing to bend a little here, we've got nowhere else to go." Jamison Price reclined casually in his imposing high-back leather chair as if he'd announced something as unimportant as the weather, not her entire future.

Alexandria Eastridge stared into his cold, calculating steel gray eyes, and she knew she should feel something—sadness, relief, something—but she was dead inside.

"You know, babe. . ." Jamison tapped his pencil against the mahogany desk.

Lexi shuddered at his intimate tone.

"A little give, a little take."

She rose, looking intently beyond Jamison out the window and across the Burbank skyline. Buildings filled with power moguls dotted her vision. "I'm through giving. Probably twelve years too late, but I'm through." She spoke the words in a quiet monotone.

"Your call, sweet thing." Though he still played it cool, Lexi didn't miss the throbbing pulse in his neck or the clenched jaw. "There's a dozen more lined up to replace you—younger, thinner, and prettier. You're a has-been, anyway." He rose and walked to the door, his height nearly dwarfing her almost six-foot frame.

He traced Lexi's jawline. "When you come to your senses, call me."

Lexi said nothing. She passed through the doorway as soon

as he opened it and stepped out of her way.

Sure enough, in the lobby sat another young teen and her mother waiting for an appointment with "Mr. Big" in the modeling world—Jamison Price. Lexi saw in the young face all the naivety she'd once possessed. All the hope. All the dreams.

"Mom, that's Alexandria." The green eyes widened as the teen whispered, gawking at Lexi.

Lexi stopped and faced the wannabe—probably only fourteen or fifteen. "It's not worth it." She shook her head. "The cost of fame is way too high," she warned. "Way too high."

Then she focused on the girl's mother. "Take her and run." Lexi turned and left the office before either had a chance to respond. She strode down the hall toward the elevators, climbing in for the ten-story ride down.

Lexi closed her eyes and leaned against the back wall. *So what now?* There was always clothing, furniture, or fragrance lines, but Lexi had this overwhelming need to walk away from this business and never look back. Maybe she'd feel differently in a few weeks.

Dazed, she exited into the parking garage and made her way to the little silver Miata. She climbed in, lowering the windows and the top. Maybe flying down the 101 to her condo in Malibu with the wind whipping through her hair would bring some sort of feeling, or maybe it would just remind her she was alive.

On the drive home, Lexi weighed her options. One overriding desire kept rising to the top. She wanted to go home. Not home to her parents' place in Beverly Hills, but home to Gram and Gramps.

Thinking of them brought a tsunami of regret and a plethora of longing. She missed them so much. They'd been the still point in her childhood, the place she felt loved, just because. She didn't have to land on any list, have her picture plastered on a magazine cover, or graduate with honors. Those things didn't matter. They just loved her—no qualifiers, no questions—just as she was.

By the time she pulled into her garage, her long locks were a ratty mess, but her plan was clear.

Once inside, the materialism mocked her. She owned the nicest things available to humanity, but what had they given her? She removed her cell phone from her Coach bag and punched the number 2. Her phone speed-dialed her grandparents—just as it did every Sunday evening—in their Nevada cabin at the south rim of Lake Tahoe.

"Hello." The sound of Gram's voice warmed her heart.

"Hi, Gram." She aimed for a chipper response.

"Lexi, it's not Sunday. Are you okay?"

"I'm fine," she lied. "I was thinking of taking a little trip up to see you."

Gram said nothing, but Lexi could tell from the sounds on the other end of the line that Gram was crying.

"Is everything okay with you?" Lexi asked.

Gram sniffed. "More than okay. It's just that you're finally coming. We've waited so long."

Lexi knew Gram meant no condemnation but was merely stating the facts. The guilt, however, pelted her like chunks of ice in a hailstorm.

"Well, I'm going to make up for lost time. How do you feel about having your guest room occupied for the rest of spring and maybe even all summer?"

"The next four or five months?" The glee Lexi heard seeping through the phone line somewhat lightened the load of guilt.

"Is that too long?" She already knew what Gram's answer would be.

"Too long? My heavens, no! It's been five years, honey. That's barely an average of two weeks a year. I'd say you owe us that." Gram laughed—that warm, happy, contagious giggle that warmed Lexi's heart.

Peace settled over her. "I'm excited, too. I'll call you later with my flight info. I can't wait to see you." She was more certain all the time that she'd made the right decision.

"Just so you know right now, I'm going to spoil you. I'll cook your favorite meals, maybe even get some meat on your bones. You're way too thin."

Lexi laughed. Gram said that almost every time they spoke. "I'll be modeling plus sizes by the end of the summer."

Her heart sank as her reality resurfaced. She'd never work as a model again. Her glory days were ending. At twenty-eight years old, she truly was a has-been.

❧

Cody Cooper backed up the wood-filled trailer next to the log home. He put the dual-wheel truck into first gear and turned off the engine, setting the emergency brake. As he exited the driver's side, Alph—his neighbor, pseudograndfather, and the truck's owner—crept out the passenger door.

"Alph, Alph!" Essie, his wife of nearly sixty years, came running around the side of the house—at least as fast as seventy-something legs could go. "Lexi's coming! Lexi's finally coming home!"

Cody's heart lurched at the news. He experienced almost as much excitement as they did.

Alph held his bride close as she cried happy tears. He grinned at Cody. "She's finally coming home. Our sweet girl is finally coming home."

Cody swallowed hard. He'd prayed for this very thing for a long time, knowing how desperately they longed to see their only grandchild again. And a part of him longed to meet her as well. He'd heard every Lexi story known to man—at least a dozen times. He'd perused Essie's scrapbook just as often, admiring the pretty baby, cute little girl, and blossoming young teen into a beautiful woman.

He could see her even now in his mind's eye. Her golden curly locks, reaching well past her shoulders, and her intense blue eyes that had grabbed his heart.

He'd seen every magazine cover she'd graced, watched a video of every runway she'd strolled, and viewed every commercial she'd shot. And somewhere in the midst of the past five years, he'd fallen in love with Lexi—not the model Alexandria Eastridge but the granddaughter who called every Sunday, the granddaughter who was cherished and loved.

But honestly he had a hard time reconciling the two. He'd seen some of the not-so-complimentary tabloid articles and the string of men she'd been associated with.

"Cody," Essie said with force.

"Huh?" He pulled out of his deep thoughts.

"Where have you been? I said your name several times." She stepped out of Alph's embrace and stood next to him.

Cody leaned against the truck fender, not willing to admit he'd been thinking about Lexi. "I'm sorry. My mind was elsewhere." He winked at Essie. "I'm listening now. What did you need?"

"Would you pick Lexi up at the airport tomorrow?"

He shrugged, acting nonchalant, though inside he was anything but. "If you need me to. I'm off. What time?"

"She called back while you two were out chopping firewood to say her plane lands in Reno tomorrow at noon.

Perhaps," Essie said as her eye got that familiar I've-got-a-great-idea glint, "the two of you could enjoy lunch together in the city before you drive her down here."

"Maybe." Cody maintained his cool attitude, not wanting to give Essie any hope. But the excitement inside him could barely be squelched.

"Possibly somewhere quiet and dimly lit so you could get to know each other without anyone recognizing her." Essie was about as subtle as firecrackers on the Fourth of July. She'd been dropping hints—well, maybe not hints so much as suggestions—for years about the wonderful couple Cody and Lexi would make. Somewhere along the way, Cody had bought into her thinking, but he never let on that he'd even be interested, since Essie was the last person he'd ever want to hurt. Sure, he agreed with her that Lexi was beautiful, but that was as far as he'd go. At least verbally.

"This is your chance, Cody. Lexi needs a strong man to love her."

"Essie!" Alph shook an index finger at the woman he loved more than life itself. "You stay out of it."

She stomped her foot. "He's perfect, and you know it."

Alph's expression grew stern. "You let Lexi and Cody alone to live their own lives."

"But neither of them have a prospect on the horizon. Cody's thirty years old, for goodness' sake. He's obviously not doing a very good job of finding someone for himself. He must need my help." Her gaze rested on Cody, daring him to deny anything she just said.

"I date." Though Cody couldn't remember if the last time had been months or more than a year.

"When?" Essie's hands rested on her hips.

He thought for a minute. "Not often, but I do."

His answer brought a smug expression to Essie's face. "The boy needs help." She crossed her arms. "If you'll both excuse me, I have a guest room to air out and spruce up." She lifted her chin and strutted away.

Cody grabbed the gloves out the truck cab he'd recently exited. "Don't worry. She doesn't bother me." He slipped his hands into the soft leather. "I'm actually flattered that she'd consider me Lexi-worthy." He moved toward the trailer.

"You know she thinks the world of you. Besides, I'm not sure Lexi is Cody-worthy."

Alph's words shocked Cody. He laid down the log he'd picked up to add to last year's dwindling stack of wood resting in the crib. "What do you mean?"

Alph's mouth was drawn into a tight line. "Just not sure what that girl of ours has been up to." Sadness filled his expression. "The world she lives in isn't a moral one."

Cody often wondered if that thought had ever crossed Alph's or Essie's mind.

"Of course, her grandmother will hear nothing of that."

Cody wasn't sure how to respond. "Maybe this is her time to return to her family and her God."

"I sure hope so. Been praying for that one a long time."

"Me, too, Alph. Me, too."

❧

Cody left Stateline, Nevada, early the next morning. Once he hit Reno, he drove his Jeep to the nearest car wash. It didn't get washed nearly as often as it needed. After it was clean and shiny, he met his brother Brady for a cup of coffee, not wanting to arrive at the airport too early.

"How's Kendall?"

"She's great." Brady grinned at the mention of his fiancée.

"You look like the cat that ate the goldfish."

"I think I am. I just can't tell you how great it is to know you're going to marry the woman of your dreams. I want that for you, dude."

Brady and Cody had always been the closest of the four siblings. Only sixteen months apart, they had an ironclad bond—always looking out for the other guy.

Standing in line to order, each purchased a large mocha frappuccino. Then they headed outside and settled at a round table shaded by an umbrella.

"So this is the big day you've been dreaming of?" Brady set his blended coffee on the table in front of him.

Cody heard the thread of disapproval in Brady's tone but chose to ignore it. "Yep." He glanced at his watch. "Just a couple of hours now."

Brady nodded and sipped his drink. Cody watched him wage a battle with himself. "Be careful, I don't want you to end up like poor Frankie."

Cody knew exactly what Brady meant. Their older brother's life was harder than it should be. His wife could be very selfish at times and pretty demanding. "You can't save her or change her—only God can do that."

Cody nodded at his older brother's wisdom, but even his well-intended warnings didn't dampen Cody's anticipation. After five years of praying, he was about to meet the girl of his dreams. Nothing—or no one—could spoil today, so he switched the subject. "And your big day isn't too far off either. What, about five weeks from now?"

A cheesy grin took up residence, and Brady nodded. That's what Cody wanted—a girl who could light up his expression and his world.

They moved on to talk about work and sports. Time crawled, and Cody kept glancing at his watch. Finally he bid his brother good-bye and headed to the airport. After parking he checked the board for Lexi's ETA and gate information. They'd be landing on time, so Cody made his way to the waiting area, watching people come and go.

Finally he spotted her coming toward him. His heart dipped as he glimpsed her in person for the very first time. She was beautiful and almost a head taller than many of the other women in the herd who made their way toward the baggage claim.

She walked with grace and purpose—her curly golden mane bounced with each step, only adding to her aura. Cody swallowed. How does a guy fall for a girl he only knows vicariously?

Her ice blue eyes searched the crowd. Their gazes met. She quickly looked down and stared at the floor as she walked.

When she passed him, he said, "Lexi?" Though she didn't respond, he knew she'd heard him. He'd seen her head jerk up, but she glanced neither right nor left and kept moving at a quick pace.

Cody followed her to the baggage claim belt, not wanting to draw undue attention to her. A few people had already seemed to recognize her and stared or whispered. Maybe it was just her presence. She was hard not to notice.

When she halted a few feet back from the baggage dispenser, Cody stopped next to her.

"Lexi, I'm Cody Coo—"

"I'm sorry, but you must have me confused with someone else." The frost in her tone was reflected in her cold stare that rested on him momentarily. "My name is not Lexi. Now, if you'll excuse me." She walked away from him to the other side of the automated belt that would soon deliver her bags.

Cody figured she was avoiding a possible pesky fan and

wasn't put off. He approached her again. "Before you dismiss me again, I'm your grandparents' neighbor and your ride home."

Disappointment settled on her features.

&

Lexi searched the crowd. *No, they wouldn't send someone else. Not after my being away this long.* But apparently they had. She didn't want to believe this guy, but there was no sign of her grandparents—not anywhere. She swallowed the mass of tears lodged in her throat, but they remained wedged against her windpipe, making normal breathing difficult.

Her shoulders drooped slightly at the realization. "I would have thought they'd pick me up themselves."

"I'm sorry. Your grandfather doesn't like to drive into Reno anymore. He hates the traffic. Besides, I think your grandmother has a little matchmaking scheme going on here." Cody smiled, but Lexi didn't return it. "She asked me to take you to lunch before we head back."

Though he seemed amused, Lexi missed the humor in that idea. "I'd prefer to go straight to their house, if you don't mind." She stood straighter, dismissing the stupid suggestion and the man who made it.

The conveyor belt started, and the first suitcase rolled out, followed by another then another.

"If you show me which bags are yours—"

"I'll get them myself." She hated the curt tone in her voice, but she couldn't leave this man with any romantic notions about her or them—no matter what schemes Gram cooked up.

Cody respected her wishes, though she instinctively knew standing by and watching her lift off six pieces of expensive and perfectly matched luggage went against his grain. She sent him to retrieve a luggage cart, and while he was gone, she scanned the crowd and checked out the airport. She'd forgotten how small and Podunk it was—not even a Starbucks in sight. They had to be at least ten or fifteen years behind in their technology. There was even a guy wearing spurs waiting for his luggage.

Lexi shook her head. This place was hick for a girl who hailed from Los Angeles. She'd gone from chic to bumpkin—all in the course of a morning. Suddenly she questioned her sanity. Was she nuts to come here?

two

Cody loaded Lexi's bags onto the cart, not attempting any more stabs at conversation. For that, Lexi was thankful. He led the way through the corridor and out into a warm, sunny day. She followed him through the parked cars until he stopped at a red Jeep Wrangler.

He placed her luggage in the back, handling it with care. What a pain to get all six pieces to fit. He opened the passenger door for her before returning the cart to its place. Lexi couldn't remember the last time a man had opened a door for her. His chivalry touched her, and a tiny fragment of ice chipped away from her attitude.

When he returned, he hopped in and started the Jeep, hooking his seat belt in the process. He never even glanced in her direction. Seemed she'd somehow offended him. No surprise. She'd become an expert at her porcupine personality. She preferred keeping everyone—and especially men—a good distance away.

The area surrounding the airport was old and dated—even the McDonald's looked last century. Cody took the 395 south. Lexi's conscience pricked and wouldn't leave her alone. After all, the guy had come all this way to pick her up. The least she could do was show some kindness. Her grandparents would be horrified.

She held most of her hair in her right hand, trying to keep the wind damage to a minimum. "So you work for my grandfather?" She yelled to be heard over the highway noise.

Cody glanced in her direction. His expression softened a tad. He was actually a nice-looking guy—wavy chocolate brown hair matched his eyes. "No. I live across the street."

"Oh. You're *that* guy." Mr. Wonderful as far as Gram was concerned. The guy did no wrong, and she never stopped talking about him. Lexi hadn't put two and two together—until now.

"So what gives with you?" Suspicion wrapped itself around each of her words.

Cody had the innocent expression down to a science. "What gives?"

"Yeah. Why are you hanging around with my grand-parents?" The accusatory tone left no doubt what she thought. She'd wondered many times during the past few years what this guy was after.

Cody pulled off the freeway at the next exit and parked in the dirt alongside the frontage road. Fear shivered down Lexi's back. She wondered if she'd be on the ten o'clock news.

"What are you implying?" A pulse hammered in Cody's jaw.

Lexi refused to back down. She'd learned that if you cower before a man, he'll walk all over you.

"How old are you?" She demanded with boldness.

"Thirty. Why?"

"And you hang around with people almost three times your age?"

"I hang around with my friends—no matter their age. What's your point?"

"I just think it's convenient that you befriend the elderly. What—are you hoping for a mention in the will?"

Cody clenched the steering wheel and sucked in a deep breath, taking his time before answering. She thought for a minute he might be praying. Then he turned and faced her.

"I moved up here for a job. I'm a fireman, and the Reno department wasn't hiring at the time. The home across from your grandparents' house had just gone up for sale." He paused.

The one they'd hoped I would buy so I could be close, at least part of each year.

"I went and saw it and signed a contract on the spot. I met your grandparents the same day. That was five years ago."

"The Reno fire department still has no openings?" Lexi raised her brow. *Oh, come on now.*

"Not that this is any of your business."

She sensed Cody growing impatient with her inference.

"I love it here. Snow ski all winter, water-ski all summer. My only regret is that I miss my family. Your grandparents fill that void for me, and since they miss you, I fill that hole for them. Like it or not, Lexi, I do care about them, and I am a part of their everyday lives."

He pulled back onto the road and onto the on-ramp. She regathered her hair, holding it tight. Cody seemed genuine, and she doubted he'd stick around for five years if he was after their money. Besides, they didn't have that much.

The freeway ended in Carson City. They followed surface roads through the historical town to the Lake Tahoe turnoff. The mountains surrounding them were barren and drab. Just piles of brown earth with no green in sight. To Lexi, they mirrored her life—piles of nothingness. After years of hard work, all she had was emptiness.

Again Lexi fought the emotions rising like a high tide and threatening to sweep over her and knock her down. Discreetly she swiped at a tear, keeping her gaze out the passenger window, staring at the mountains that mocked her. Upon closer inspection, they were covered with a golden, dead-looking grass and small shrubs.

As the road climbed higher, the mountains grew more beautiful. Lexi began to spot life, and trees appeared. The road curved back and forth, and the mountains became dense with pines. Sadly, some of the hillsides carried scars from fires that had left them charred. Another thing they had in common—scars.

The picture planted a seed of hope in Lexi's heart. Maybe here she, too, could find life in the deadness of her soul. Maybe newness might bloom in her scarred and broken heart.

As they rolled over the top of another hill, Lexi caught her first glimpse of Lake Tahoe, and as always, it took her breath away. A tiny gasp escaped.

"It does that to me, too. Every single time. That's why I'm still here."

A million emotions churned inside as she watched the sun dance across the lake, leaving a glistening glow behind. In every direction, majestic mountains stood guard over the body of water. And Lexi's heart cried for home. After running from herself, God, and her shame, she was finally almost there.

Without warning, a dam broke. Tears she'd stored for years burst through, and a deluge ran down her cheeks, dropping off her chin and onto her silk blouse.

❧

Cody knew the moment her emotions gave way. He could hear it in her breathing, and he hurt for her. "Would you like me to stop?"

She kept her focus out the windshield, shaking her head no and sniffing.

He popped open the glove box, leaning across her and catching a whiff of a subtle fragrance. He handed her a napkin.

"It's no Kleenex, but it's all I've got."

"Thanks."

She dabbed at her face. He knew from his mom and sister that she hoped to preserve as much of her makeup as possible. By the time he turned into her grandparents' drive, she'd pulled herself together and touched up a few places with a new layer of cosmetics, but there was no hiding the red-rimmed eyes or the Rudolph-looking nose.

Alph and Essie were out their front door before he even rolled to a stop, and Lexi was out of the Jeep and into their arms before his seat belt was undone.

Cody left them in their tearful huddle, making two trips to the guest room with Lexi's luggage. She'd apparently come to stay. Just about every piece of clothing he owned—along with much of the contents of his home—would fit into her bags.

The three of them were just coming into the house as he was leaving. "Cody," Essie grabbed his arm and pulled him back inside with them. "Let me feed you lunch. It's the least we can do. Lexi says she didn't want to stop, and you must be hungry. It's almost two."

He glanced at Lexi, but her expression gave him no indication of her desires. Her arm was intertwined with her grandfather's, and they walked together toward the kitchen.

Cody stopped and gently freed himself from Essie's grip. "I think I should give you guys some time alone."

"Baloney." She grabbed his arm and pulled him toward the kitchen. "Alph, will you please tell Cody that we don't need space from him? He's like family, after all."

Essie's announcement brought Lexi to attention. She was suddenly very interested in what was being said. Her gaze rested on him.

"Be that as it may, I've got some things to do this afternoon."

And your granddaughter doesn't want me hanging around. Cody kissed Essie's cheek and winked at her. Then he gave Alph the handshake and half hug they always shared. "Lexi." He couldn't exactly say it was a pleasure. "I'm sure I'll see you around."

"Probably at breakfast tomorrow," Gram threw in.

Lexi's eyes widened, but she held her tongue.

"Cody does most of our chores these days, and in return, we often feed him breakfast or dinner." Alph filled her in on their arrangement. No one actually planned it, but this was what their relationship had morphed into. They fed him, and he helped them. Seemed perfect until today. Somehow, Lexi's raised eyebrows made it feel wrong. She clearly disapproved. He decided he'd best stay away as much as they'd allow. He didn't want to hurt their feelings, but they'd probably get busy with that granddaughter of theirs and not notice much anyway.

After Lexi insisted that her gram let him leave, if that was what he wanted, Cody headed across the street to his A-frame cabin, relieved to have some time to ponder today's events.

His cell phone rang just as he turned off the Jeep. Brady's name scrolled across his screen. Cody flipped it open. "Hey, bro."

"Hey. I was thinking that I might have been a little harsh this morning. Talk about raining on your parade and all."

"It's okay. Your advice was well intended."

"You sound down. You all right?"

"Yeah. . .I guess. . .I don't know." Cody decided to bare his soul to his brother. "Here's the deal: I've spent the last five years listening to all these stories about this wonderful Christian girl."

"And somehow you fell for her." Brady cut to the heart of the matter.

"Was I that obvious?" Cody opened the fridge, wishing he

kept it better stocked.

"Yep. You talk about her all the time."

"I do?" Cody thought about that. She was on his mind fairly often. "I guess I do." He pulled out some leftover pot roast Essie had sent home with him and popped it in the microwave. "Anyway, the girl I picked up at the airport this afternoon in no way resembles the Lexi in her grandparents' renditions."

"I suppose I'm not surprised, but I feel bad for you, man."

Cody hit the REHEAT button. "Well, stupidly I was surprised. Her cool distance and borderline rudeness caught me off guard."

"Of course her grandparents would think she's wonderful, but don't they ever glance at those magazines when they're checking out at the grocery store?"

"I guess they assumed—just as I did—that it's all publicity fodder. But the word *shrew*, which I've seen attached to her name more than once, was true of the girl I just dropped off across the street."

"Whoa, that's harsh, bro."

The microwave shut off and beeped, indicating that Cody's lunch was hot. "All I can say is, she's nothing like her grandparents painted her to be. And the sad thing is—the joke's on me, because for all intents and purposes, I'm half in love with a figment of someone else's imagination. If that's not irony, I don't know what is." Cody chuckled at the sheer nuttiness of it all. But truth be told, he had no idea what to do with all the feelings he had regarding a Lexi who didn't exist.

❧

Relief washed over Lexi when Gram finally let Cody leave without too much of a fuss. After Lexi changed into a pair of khaki shorts and a sleeveless top, she set the table while

Gram heated up the chicken enchiladas that she had made earlier to serve for dinner that night. "We'll just eat these twice today." Gram set the piping hot pan on a trivet in the center of the table. "They're your favorites anyway."

"Yes, they are." Lexi took her seat and unfolded her napkin, placing it in her lap. "It's my fault we didn't stop for lunch. Cody offered, but lunching with a complete stranger didn't appeal to me." She smiled at her grandparents. "I'd much rather be here with the two of you."

"Honey, Cody is no stranger." Gram served up two enchiladas onto Lexi's plate. "He is quite dear to your gramps and me."

"That may be so, but he's a stranger to me." Lexi took her first bite, savoring the spicy green sauce blanketing the chicken, tortillas, and jack cheese. "These are as good as I remember." She smiled at Gram.

"I promised to spoil you and put some meat on those bones."

Lexi finished the end of the sentence with her, and they laughed. She couldn't recall the last time she'd felt so carefree. Yes, coming was a good decision—except for the Cody part. Eating with him every day might prove difficult. She'd help her grandparents see the light as far as he was concerned.

"That neighbor fellow of yours—what gives with him?"

Both of her grandparents frowned and glanced at each other. "What in the world do you mean, child?" Gramps asked.

"You don't think it's a little strange that a thirty-year-old guy hangs out with the two of you?" Lexi horrified herself with how awful she sounded. "I didn't mean that badly. It's just that most people hang out with other people close to their own age. Is he some sort of freak or something?"

"Lexi!" Gram's tone was shocked. "Do not speak of Cody in

such a way. And to think I'd hoped you two would hit it off!"

Well, at least we've settled that one.

Gramps laid down his fork and gave Lexi his full attention. "That's the problem with you young people. Few of you know the value of multigenerational relationships. Friends are far more important to most of you than family."

Lexi knew the conversation had shifted from Cody to her, but she didn't have the courage to tell them it wasn't friends but shame that had kept her away all these years.

"As we've aged, Cody's been a dear to have around. There are so many chores we just can't do anymore." Gram spoke quietly, her eyes begging Lexi to give Cody half a chance. "He's literally a godsend."

"Aging without loved ones nearby creates hardship for older folks." Gramps rested his elbows on the table, and his hands were intertwined near his chin. "When Cody moved up here, he knew no one and missed his family something fierce. We each had a need that could be filled by the other. And your gram loved having someone other than me to cook for."

"He kind of filled a place in our lives that you couldn't, so we'd appreciate your being kind to him." Gram's tone was no-nonsense, but her eyes were filled with hurt.

With Lexi's emotions so near the surface, it was a battle not to cry again. "I'm sorry. I have let you down, and so have my parents. Don't worry—I'll be on my best behavior, for your sake." She smiled and blinked several times, keeping her tears at bay. Her gaze rested on Gram. "However, please no matchmaking. He's not my type; nor am I his. *I'm sure he's way too nice for me.* "How about if after lunch we go for a walk? Remember where you took me last time on that peak where we could see out over the whole lake? Let's go there again."

After the table was cleared and the dishes stowed in the dishwasher, the three of them made their way out the door and started hiking toward Lexi's favorite peak.

Though her grandparents were nearing eighty, they were in pretty good health. Walking two or three miles a day had been their practice since Lexi was a small child, and they were still doing it. The pace may have slowed, but they could still follow a trail up the mountainside.

During the walk, they were all more contemplative than talkative. Lexi was grateful for the silence and the time to think more about Cody. He seemed genuine. And they really loved him. But the relationship still didn't add up in Lexi's mind.

When they finally reached the lookout, the sun hung low in the western sky. Something about the lake always beckoned to Lexi. They each settled onto a boulder and took in the view. No one needed to talk. They just breathed in the fresh mountain air and rested.

No smog. No crowds. No traffic. Just peace.

Then Cody's face rose to the forefront of her mind, and her peace was shattered. How would she spend every day in his presence and be kind at the same time? Why did she have such strong feelings of dislike toward him? She'd get to the bottom of whatever was really going on. She'd expose Cody as the fraud she suspected him to be.

three

Lexi opened her eyes and lay staring at the ceiling. She hadn't slept well again and awoke feeling tired. She'd tossed and turned much of the night.

She thought about the past two weeks. She'd done little except hike the mountains and grieve over the mess she'd made of her life. She'd sold herself out for a dozen years of fame that led to nothing but emptiness and regret.

She had no real friends. Oh sure, she'd received many messages on her cell phone these past fourteen days. All from men. Men who wanted to take her to some party or event and flash her around as arm candy. Many were old enough to be her dad, and not one of them cared about her—about the real her, the woman inside. All they cared about was how she looked and that she slept with them at the end of the night.

A tear rolled down her cheek. As a teen, she'd promised God to wait. Somewhere in the back of one of her jewelry boxes was a purity ring that her grandparents had given her on her thirteenth birthday after she'd gone forward at a teen conference and made that commitment.

The guy she'd waited for never showed up, but at times, her bed felt like a revolving door. Each time emptier and less satisfying than the one before.

Several more tears rolled from her eyes and into her hair. At first all the attention had been fun, but even at sixteen, it didn't take her long to figure out they only wanted her body. By the time she was out of her teens, she'd lost count of the men, but she had learned the motto of the business well. *You scratch my back, and I'll scratch yours.* If she hadn't given them what they wanted, she'd never have gone as far in the modeling world or experienced the success she'd known. But in the end, the cost was far too high. If only she'd known at sweet sixteen what she did now.

Lexi rose, wiping her cheeks with her palms. She headed for the shower, hoping to wash away the memories but knowing all the while the act was futile.

Lexi was relieved to find Cody's chair vacant this morning when she glanced out the window to the table on the patio on her way to the kitchen for coffee. He'd been scarce the past fourteen days, and she was glad. He'd actually only dined with them a couple of times, and they didn't interact much with one another. He seemed as bent on avoiding her as she was him.

"I just finished making your omelet." Gram handed her a plate. "Spinach and Swiss. Gramps is still out at the table reading the paper and finishing his coffee. Why don't you join him on the deck?"

Lexi loved that her grandparents ate most meals outdoors. That was something she rarely did in LA.

She carried her breakfast and coffee, taking the seat next to Gramps. Gram followed her out with a small glass of fresh orange juice.

"They're saying that fire yesterday was arson." Gramps looked up from the paper at the two of them.

"I don't get it. Who would do something like that?" Lexi stirred cream into her coffee—an indulgence she'd never allowed herself before.

"And why so close to people's homes? If it hadn't been extinguished so quickly, some of our friends and neighbors might have lost everything." Gram walked over and stood behind Gramps, reading over his shoulder.

" 'Several witnesses report seeing a young woman in the area,'" she read. " 'The police are working with the fire marshal to identify the woman and bring her in for questioning.' Probably one of those high school girls who dresses in all black and wears the weird makeup."

"Just because kids look different these days doesn't make them bad," Lexi said.

"Well, they look bad to me." Gram shook her head. "Anyway, I hope they catch her and she gets all she deserves and more." Gram carried Gramps' empty plate into the kitchen.

❧

Cody read the report from the fire marshal, and his heart sank. The suspect was described as a woman in her twenties with blond curly hair and very tall. He read each witness's account, and though many things varied, each one said the woman was tall and her hair was long and curly. "Dear God, please don't let it be so."

He'd already resigned himself to the fact that Lexi wasn't the Lexi he'd fallen for. He barely tolerated the real Lexi, but surely she couldn't be an arsonist. That would kill her grandparents. He read the report again. The facts were hard to deny. He'd pop in for lunch and see what Lexi had been up to.

He rapped twice on his neighbors' kitchen door and let himself in. "Cody, what a surprise!" Essie kissed his cheek. "You're just in time for lunch. Can you spare a half hour or so? You've been awfully busy lately. Are you avoiding us or our granddaughter?" Essie was never one to hide her true thoughts.

Cody thought about his answer and decided he'd go with

the "Honesty is the best policy" theory. "I know you hoped Lexi and I would have chemistry, and we do. We both rub each other the wrong way." Cody chuckled. "I'm sorry, but those are the facts."

Essie nodded and pulled another plate from the cupboard, setting it next to the two others at the bar.

"Where's Lexi?"

"She's out hiking," Alph said as he settled on one of the high chairs at the three-person bar. "Packs her lunch every day and is gone for hours."

More facts stacked up against her. "Every day?" Cody probed.

"Just about." Essie placed a smoked trout salad in front of him. "She didn't hike on her first couple of days here or either Sunday."

Alph nodded. "Both Sundays we all came home from church, ate a big lunch, and took long siestas." He paused to bless the food before they ate.

Cody felt sick. No wonder so many people reported spotting her. She's out walking every single day to God only knew where. "It's not considered safe to hike alone. Do you think it's a good idea?" He took a forkful of lettuce and trout.

"Lexi says the wilderness is much safer than the wilds of LA, and she is probably right. She takes plenty of food, water, her cell phone, and a compass. She also wears one of those big floppy-brimmed hats and sunglasses that cover 75 percent of her face."

Her cell phone was useless in much of the surrounding area. Cody knew that for a fact. "Does she at least tell you where she's going?"

"That she does," Alph chimed in. "Today she is hiking down to Zephyr Cove to swim in the lake."

Great, swimming alone isn't good, either. He wanted to say, "Don't you people get the danger she's putting herself in?" But he didn't bother. Both Essie and Alph seemed nonchalant and unconcerned about Lexi's welfare.

And today she'd gone right down past fire station number three—his firehouse. She'd probably marched right by it on Elk's Cove Road, not having any idea that someone might spot her and notice her description fits the arsonist to a tee. He ate quickly, planning to head down there and read her the riot act.

He hugged Alph and Essie, thanked them for lunch, and hopped in his Jeep. He prayed the entire four miles to the cove. "Please, Lord, reveal who really set the fires and don't let it be Lexi. Her grandparents have served You faithfully for years. For their sake, Lord, let it be anybody but her." But he knew that like everyone, Lexi had a free will, and God allowed all people to choose for themselves.

Cody parked and headed down to the lake. He spotted her lying on the beach in a modest, black, one-piece suit—her golden hair fanned out around her. A longing hit him. How he wished she'd been the girl of his dreams. He'd never met a more beautiful woman, but it was the inside that mattered most to him. And there, it seemed, Lexi sadly lacked.

❧

Lexi lay on her bright, oversized towel in the beach area. There were a few other swimmers and sunbathers but not many.

As a model, her tan had been the spray-on kind. Her manager forbade sunning due to possible skin damage. For all practical purposes, he'd owned her.

"Lexi." The deep, quiet voice startled her. She jerked to a sitting position. It took a minute for her eyes to adjust to the brightness of the day. She shaded them and squinted. Cody stood a couple of feet from her.

"May I join you?"

Her stomach knotted. She thought they'd reached an understanding and sort of had an unspoken agreement. She assumed their dislike was mutual, so why was he here, ruining her perfectly peaceful afternoon?

"It's important."

She rose to her feet, pulling a wrap over her suit. "Are my grandparents okay?"

He nodded. "It's not them I'm worried about. Where did you hike yesterday?"

"One Hundred Dollar Saddle lookout. Why?"

"Did you hear about yesterday's grass fire?"

She pulled her brows together, trying to remember. "Yeah—sort of. Gram and Gramps were reading an article about it this morning. I wasn't really paying much attention, though. Why?"

He seemed extremely serious and was watching her closely—almost studying her—like one would a bug under a microscope. "Several people reported spotting you in the area."

"Yeah, so?" She shrugged. "I just told you I hiked near there." Now she considered him as intently as he had her.

"You're the *only* person anyone saw anywhere near the area."

Suddenly his implications were clear. Lexi's heart constricted, and fear settled on her like a blanket on a cold evening. The weight of it covered her. "You don't think. . ." Her tone was incredulous. Dizziness overtook her, and she sat back down.

"It doesn't make a difference what I think." His expression

was matter-of-fact. He bent down on one knee in front of her, leaning in mere inches from her face. "Did you set that fire?" he asked slowly, enunciating each word. His eyes mirrored the uncertainty of his voice.

"Of course not! Is that what you think? Is that what they think?" She pulled her wrap tighter around her. "Cody, it's not true! You have to believe me!"

But why should he? She'd accused him of something just as bad—using her elderly grandparents. "Please." She closed her eyes momentarily, gulping in a deep breath. She licked her dry lips. "I know you don't think very highly of me, and rightly so. I haven't been very nice, but I'm not a criminal. I'd never do anything like that." She shook her head, horror etched across her face.

She didn't do it. He was sure of it. Her response was pure, unadulterated shock.

"I can't believe this is happening. Do my grandparents think I started the fire?" Her breathing was heavy and slightly erratic.

"They don't even know you're a suspect."

"Cody, I didn't do it." Her eyes pleaded with him to believe her. Her hand quivered as she laid it across her mouth. She squeezed her eyes shut.

"I believe you."

She dropped her hand and opened her eyes. "You do?" Relief flooded her face. "You really do?" Now she studied him.

He nodded.

"Why? Why would you believe me?"

"I don't know. I just feel it in my gut. Either you're a top-notch actress or you're telling the truth. I'm going with the latter." Cody rose to his feet and offered her a hand, pulling her up with him.

"What do we do now?" she asked on the walk back to his Jeep. Funny how they'd suddenly become a "we."

"You need to lay low for a few days. Maybe there's another tall, curly headed blond around somewhere." Cody opened the passenger door for Lexi. "The police are only collecting information at this point, so there is no warrant or anything."

Cody climbed into the driver's seat and started the engine. "My guess is, it's a case of being in the wrong place at the wrong time. The real arsonist was much more discreet and remained unseen. Please don't hike alone anymore. At least not until this is resolved."

Lexi nodded her agreement. "I won't."

Cody drove her home and walked her to the door.

She paused before going inside, turning to face him. "Thank you for believing me. I couldn't blame you if you didn't."

Their gazes locked. Feelings for the imagined Lexi and newfound compassion for this one collided inside him. He longed to pull her into his arms, assure her everything would be okay, and kiss all the fear away. He, however, did nothing but stand there gawking. She did the same. He wondered if she felt the emotions he did—the unmistakable chemistry, the undeniable pull.

❧

For a moment, Lexi thought Cody might kiss her, and for a moment, the idea didn't repulse her. Instead, he shoved his hands into the front pockets of his jeans and took a couple of steps backward. She swallowed, and the moment dissipated. All that remained was an awkwardness.

"I better get inside."

He nodded his agreement.

She needed to say something more to him, but nothing came.

"Well, see ya." He took another step away from her.

"Bye." She watched him saunter to his Jeep. Once inside, he waved. She did the same and let herself into the house.

Nothing but silence greeted her. Her grandparents must be catching their afternoon nap. She tiptoed to her room, hoping the wood floor wouldn't creak. She needed some time alone and was thankful her room was at the opposite end of the house from theirs.

Lexi changed into a pair of sweats and an oversized T-shirt. She slipped her feet into warm, fuzzy slippers and perched on the side of her bed, picking up the Bible Gram always left on the guest room nightstand.

"It's been a long time." The tears she'd held at bay since Cody's surprise visit refused to lie dormant a moment longer. An army of them marched down her cheeks. At first she tried to swipe them away, but since her efforts were futile, she let them fall where they might.

She grabbed the box of tissues that sat next to where the Bible had been and lay back across her bed, eyes on the ceiling. She pulled a couple of tissues from the box and dried her face then set the box next to her on the bed and laid the Bible on her chest, hugging it against her heart.

"God, it's me, Lexi. Do You still remember who I am?" The words, nothing more than a coarse whisper, sounded silly. "Of course You do. I recall learning that somewhere in the Bible it says I'm the apple of Your eye and my name is engraved on the palm of Your hand. So I know You haven't forgotten me."

Lexi cried harder. How could God still love her? Yet she knew He did. And somehow she knew He was calling her, softly and tenderly, back to Him. Sunday in church, she'd felt that old familiar tug on her heart. He'd gone after that one stray sheep she'd learned years ago in children's church. And this time, the stray was her.

As Lexi thought back over the last dozen years and the many compromises she'd made along the way, she felt physically sick. Curled into a ball on the bed, she recited all the acts she could remember and asked God to forgive each one.

Finally, after she'd laid herself bare before Him, a mantle of peace settled over her like she hadn't known in years. One more thing nagged her conscience, so after she washed her face, she slipped out the sliding door to her private patio and headed across the street. Cody's Jeep sat parked out front, so she was certain he'd be there.

She lifted her chin and forced herself to knock on the door.

&

Cody went to the door expecting to see Alph, but there stood a fragile-looking Lexi. She'd been crying hard, as her splotchy face, red nose, and swollen eyes testified.

He swung his door open wide. "Would you like to come in?"

She nodded but stopped just inside the doorway, facing him. "I'm sort of making things right with God today, and I felt the need to do the same with you."

"Do you want to sit down?" Cody motioned toward a leather sofa facing a stone fireplace.

She moved toward the couch, and he followed, taking an oversized chair kitty-corner to her. She folded her hands in her lap, staring at them for several seconds. Then she raised her gaze to meet his, sucked in a deep breath, and sent him a tiny, embarrassed smile. "I'm sorry that I've been horrible to you ever since I arrived. I don't have a very good track record with men and struggle to trust or like most of your kind."

Her confession brought an ache to Cody's heart. Probably much of what he'd read about her was true. Men used her and threw her away.

"I forgive you, Lexi." And he did. More lines blurred between the Lexi he'd heard about for years and this one sitting before him. Right now, in her vulnerability, she was precious to him.

four

"So you're a Christian?"

She laughed a self-conscious laugh. "I'm sure it was hard to tell, but I once was."

"Then you still are."

"I've wandered pretty far." Lexi picked up one of his sofa pillows and hugged it against her chest.

"When did you become a Christ follower?"

"I was just a little girl—probably six or seven. I asked Jesus into my heart at vacation Bible school."

Cody wasn't sure how much he should ask, but he wanted to know. "So what happened then?"

"My parents are atheists. My mom is my grandparents' only child. I guess they were pretty strict with her when she was growing up, and once she got out of the house, she wanted nothing to do with church or God and little to do with them."

Cody nodded, hoping to encourage her to continue. He knew bits and pieces but didn't know the whole story.

"I've heard Gram say more than once that she wished they'd emphasized God was a loving Father who wanted a relationship and not a set of rules to follow." Lexi seemed a million miles away. "Anyway, I grew up in Beverly Hills. My parents were part of the movie scene—my mom directed and my dad produced. That was their dream for me. I failed them, too." Lexi gazed into the fireplace.

"I started taking acting classes when I was three, but I was never any good. I got a reprieve every summer when they shipped me off to stay with Gram and Gramps. That's when they reinforced the spiritual side of my life.

"Finally, when I was a sophomore in high school, my parents let go of the acting idea and pursued modeling instead. My career took off fairly quickly, and they'd finally found a way to make me *somebody*." Her voice cracked with emotion.

Cody knew by her last statement that she'd never felt loved or accepted until she had a recognizable name and face.

"Why in the world am I boring you with my life story?"

"I'm not bored, I promise. It's a world most of us only read about, but few live in it."

"The lucky few." Sarcasm enveloped those three words, and Cody knew Lexi felt anything but lucky.

"What happened with God?"

Lexi met his gaze, her eyes sad. "At the ripe old age of fifteen, I got caught up in the whole idea of fame and fortune and chased the modeling dream. I left Him behind eating my dust." Lexi hesitated, and he wasn't sure she'd continue. She picked at the yarn on the pillow in her lap.

She cleared her throat. "Shortly after my sixteenth birthday, my manager promised me if I did him a few favors he'd make sure I made it to the top. So I compromised my beliefs and myself to climb the elusive ladder of success."

Lexi raised her gaze to meet his. "And as they say, the rest is history."

He reached over and took her hand—his heart aching for her and all she'd been through. "I'm so sorry. No man had the right to use you like that." Cody had an urge to hunt the guy down and pound him into the ground for the shame he'd caused her.

She pulled her hand away. "He didn't force me. I'd failed miserably at acting, so I needed the successes. My parents wanted me to achieve. He offered an opportunity, and I grabbed it with both eyes wide open. For a while, I even convinced myself I was in love with him. That way it didn't seem so cheap and sleazy."

Lexi shook her head and laughed. She rose from the couch. "My goodness—talk about more than you bargained for. I've never shared my story with anyone before."

Cody rose, too. "I'm glad I could be the first, and your secrets are safe with me." He followed her to the front door.

She paused before opening it and faced him. "Would you come to dinner tonight? Gram mopes every time you don't."

He chuckled. "Sure."

"I know you basically changed your whole routine because of me. I promise I'll behave *if* you'll return to the way things were between you and my grandparents."

Cody nodded. "Lexi, I'm not using them or out to take advantage of them. I'm just a man who loves family, and they needed one."

Lexi hung her head. "I know. And thank you." She returned her gaze to his. "You filled a void that needed filling. I'm sorry I said such awful things to you. Will you forgive that as well?"

"I will."

❧

During the next couple of weeks, Lexi reacquainted herself with God through a daily time of devotional reading and prayer. Cody loaned her his copy of *The Purpose-Driven Life*, which for her was a refresher course in God 101. Church still felt exactly the same, only the crowd was much older than before. They still sang the old hymns she'd grown up singing, and her favorite was still "Softly and Tenderly Jesus Is Calling." But the messages always felt more relevant than when she was a kid.

She also heeded Cody's advice and never went anywhere alone. But because of that promise Cody had evoked from her, he ended up spending most of his time off hiking with her. On the days he couldn't, she and Gram took long walks or short hikes. Things with Cody went back to the way they were pre-Lexi, so he was around a lot. Gram was as content as a kitten living in a pool of cream.

Lexi and Gram were almost home from their morning walk when she commented, "You and Cody are sure becoming chummy."

Lexi raised her brows and glanced sideways at Gram. "Chummy?" Lexi shook her head. "We're becoming friends, and I haven't had a real friend in a very long time." Her famous friends came and went, but none were trustworthy. They'd use whomever they needed to gain another rung up the ladder of success.

"But don't you go getting any ideas, Gram. We are friends. Period. There is absolutely no hope for romance." Lexi doubted her heart could ever trust or love again. And Cody deserved someone way better than her.

❧

Cody wasn't on duty today and planned to hike with Lexi later in the afternoon. She and Essie had taken an early morning walk and invited him, but he had some things he needed to get done.

His cell phone rang, and he picked it up off the snack bar dividing his kitchen and living room. It was one of his buddies down at the station. "Hey, Chip."

"You asked me to call if there were more grass fires. One

was set this morning not too far from those expensive cabins off Mendon Road."

Cody leaned against his kitchen counter, letting out a long sigh. "What time?"

"Early. Before seven. One of the neighbors spotted the same woman described previously just minutes before she smelled the smoke."

"The tall blond?"

"Yep."

His heart crashed to the floor. "Was she alone?"

"The report doesn't say."

"Any idea about the course of action?"

"The captain said the authorities didn't really pursue the first one, but a second fire with the same MO and suspect? He doubts they'll let this one slide. Sounds to me like some pretty little girl got bored."

Cody's stomach curled, and it was all he could do not to defend Lexi's honor. *Why was she out walking alone? She'd promised.* "Anything else?"

"Naw. Just the usual concerns. Setting the side of a hill on fire is bad enough, but when you're only a couple of football fields from someone's home, that's another matter."

"It sure is. Thanks for filling me in."

"What's your interest in this case anyway?"

Cody paused, scrambling for an answer. "Since it's out in my neck of the woods, I'm concerned. I haven't forgotten the last loon from a couple of years ago over by Meeks Bay. He started at a distance and got closer and closer to homes until several cabins ended up taking a hit."

"That's why the captain thinks they'll put out a warrant sooner than later."

Cody closed his eyes against the onslaught of bad news and

said a quick prayer for Lexi and her grandparents. "Thanks for the update. I'll keep my eyes open. If you hear anything else—"

"Call," Chip finished.

Cody shut his cell phone, laying it back on the counter. He mulled over the info for several minutes and had no idea what to think. His mind couldn't wrap around everything and make sense of it, but he sure hoped Lexi hadn't been alone this morning.

Glancing out the window, the large home sitting across the street looked just like it always did. He decided to check things out for himself.

Alph answered his knock on the front door. He opened the door wide. "Cody, come in. I think Essie still has some warm coffee in the pot. You need a cup?"

"Nope. I'm good, but thanks. I thought I'd see what everybody has been up to today."

He followed Alph into the family room.

"Lexi and Essie took their usual sunrise walk. My hip's still giving me fits, so I stayed home and spent some extra time studying for my Sunday school lesson. Our class is in Job, and I want to teach the passage in a way that honors God."

Cody glanced at the stack of commentaries and Bibles next to Alph's chair. The man took the Word seriously.

"Where's Lexi and Essie?"

"Out puttering in the garden. Go on out." He motioned to the sliding glass door.

Cody sauntered outside and paused on the porch, watching grandmother and granddaughter work side by side—their backs toward him. Lexi wore one of Gram's straw hats with a big brim. He wondered if anyone would ever believe that a supermodel enjoyed digging in the earth, nurturing and growing vegetables and flowers.

Just the sight of her warmed his heart. He'd fallen in love with her all over again as they hiked, talked, and laughed. There really wasn't much difference between the real deal and the one her grandparents talked about. He saw more and more of the original as he got to know her better. It seemed the fires had brought with them brokenness and humility. The frost had melted.

"How was your walk this morning?" he asked as he stepped off the porch.

Both turned their heads to see him.

"Wonderful, as always." Essie rose and brushed the dirt off her hands. "I always imagined that models slept until noon, but Lexi assures me that their rigorous schedule included very early days in order to get their hair and makeup done and ready for the next shoot. That explains why she's always up at the crack of dawn."

Lexi rose. "Gram, like everyone, assumes models live a life of luxury and pampering." A smudge of dirt streaked her cheek.

He longed to take the few steps necessary and wipe it off but instead shoved his hand into the front pocket of his jeans. "Hey, you've already convinced me they don't." He focused on Essie. "Those girls really do work hard. Many twelve-hour days. Hot lights. Hours with a personal trainer. Not much time for a life." Cody parroted the facts he'd learned from Lexi during the past weeks.

Lexi got in his face, one hand on her hip and the other shaking an index finger near his nose. "Are you mocking me, buster?"

Cody shook his head in an exaggerated motion. "Nope. No mocking. Just quoting a famous model I once knew."

He grabbed her finger and used his to poke at her ribs. She squealed and laughed.

Essie watched their playful banter with delight filling her expression.

Uh-oh. She's taking this in a direction it will never actually head. Lexi has zero interest in me, Cody thought.

❧

Lexi followed the direction of Cody's gaze, realizing they'd given Gram the wrong impression. She'd have to set her straight, because there was more chance of snow in July than her ever settling down and marrying anyone—and definitely never a guy with a spotless past like Cody seemed to have.

They'd both taken a few steps away from the other, and an uncomfortable moment hung between them. Gram gazed from one to the other, watching with anticipation.

Cody recovered first. "I almost forgot why I came by. How would you like to go on a drive around the lake today?"

His suggestion brought a smile. "I'd love to. I haven't done that in years." She glanced at Essie. "I was just a little girl last time, and nothing was more boring than a seventy-two-mile drive around a lake that I'd rather have been in than viewing from a car window. Maybe I'll appreciate it more this time around." She headed for the back door. "I'll wash up and be ready in a few." Stopping at the door, she turned back. Her gaze rested on Gram. "You don't mind, do you?"

"Me?" She waved her hand as if to rid Lexi of such a ridiculous idea. "Of course not."

I bet you don't, you little matchmaker you.

When Lexi returned a few minutes later, Gram had packed water bottles and lemonade in a small ice chest. Cody grabbed the ice chest, and Lexi led the way out to his Jeep. This time she was prepared; she'd pulled her hair into a ponytail.

Cody drove out to Highway 50 and turned left. In less than two minutes, they'd crossed the state line and were in California. Just past the border, Cody pointed out the Heavenly ski resort gondola.

"It was pretty new the last time I was here. Promise not to laugh?"

Cody nodded his agreement.

"When my grandparents mentioned they were putting in a gondola, I imagined little boats with singing Italian men—not a ski lift up the mountain."

Cody tried not to break his promise but ended up being unable to contain his mirth. "Seriously?"

"Seriously. And might I mention, you're laughing." She really didn't mind. She loved the sound of his rich, timbered chuckle.

Cody pulled into the Starbucks in South Lake Tahoe, just past the base of the gondola. "I figure an LA girl must be dying for chic coffee. What can I get you?"

"You remembered." He sure knew how to impress a girl. On one of their walks, she mentioned her Starbucks fetish. He opened her door and the door to the coffee shop. "Your mama taught you well."

"It was actually my dad. I think some things are caught rather than taught."

They got in line to order.

Lexi realized they'd spent hours talking about modeling—a safe and nonpersonal topic—but very little time talking about him. And though she tried hard to forget, she'd shared with him, and only him, her deepest, darkest secrets. Things she wished she could erase. But a lightness and freshness had come as a result of confessing her past to someone other than just God.

Cody ordered a large mocha frappuccino.

"A tall skinny mocha latte," Lexi said.

The guy eyed her up and down. "Do I know you?"

Lexi shook her head. "I don't think so. I'm not from this area."

Cody handed him a ten.

Another couple pointed and whispered. She heard them say, "Alexandria." Turning away, she whispered to Cody, "I'll meet you at the car."

He handed her the keys. "I've got a cap and some extra sunglasses in the glove box." He'd bent his head low and spoke softly right next to her ear. His breath danced across her neck, sending shivers down her spine.

"Thanks."

She loved his intuitive nature. He never seemed to miss or forget a thing. Digging through her Coach bag, she pulled out an oversized pair of sunglasses. They covered a good portion of her face, which was the goal. Taking Cody's Anaheim Angels cap from the glove box, she adjusted the back strap and pulled it low on her head. Glancing in the mirror, she decided no one would recognize her now. She barely recognized herself.

Cody joined her in a couple of minutes, handing her the hot drink.

"Cody, tell me about you, your family, and what you've been doing the past thirty years," she said as he pulled back onto the highway.

He shrugged. "Not much to tell." He pointed to a road labeled HIGHWAY 50 that curved to the left. "The Lake Tahoe airport is that way. I was surprised you didn't fly there instead of Reno."

"This girl doesn't like those little planes. No thank you. But I'm confused. I thought we were on Highway 50."

"Believe it or not, there are three different highway numbers on this one road that circles the whole lake. Highway 50 took off toward the little airport, and now we are on 89. At Tahoe City, this takes off toward Truckee, and we'll suddenly be on Highway 28."

"So what do you actually know about Lake Tahoe? Since you're unwilling to talk about yourself, we might as well see who has more useless facts stored up here." Lexi pointed to her head.

"I know we are almost to Camp Richardson. And I know for certain if this was a game of Jeopardy and the category was Lake Tahoe, I'd win." His glance in her direction reeked of smugness.

"I think not. Did you know this lake is twenty-two miles long and twelve miles wide?"

He furrowed his brow for a moment. "I think I did know that. And did you know this is considered the most beautiful drive in America?"

"Not when you're twelve."

He chuckled. "No, I suppose not."

five

"There's the Forest Service Visitor Center." Cody pointed out the next landmark.

"You read that on the sign. It doesn't count toward our contest to see who knows this lake the best." She used a schoolteacher voice, sounding authoritarian.

Cody pulled into the Emerald Bay lookout. "This is one of the most photographed places in the world, and I'm seeing it with one of the most photographed women in the world." He opened her door again.

She lowered her gaze. "Hardly. I'm small potatoes compared to Tyra Banks and the likes of her."

"You're far more beautiful." Cody's voice took on a husky quality.

Their gazes locked, and Lexi found the simple act of breathing suddenly difficult. Men often told her that, but with Cody, it was different. He was sincere. Today the words meant something to her, and they never had before.

She broke eye contact and didn't respond but admired the beauty in silence, a tenderness settling over her. If she let herself, falling for Cody Cooper would be so easy. Her gaze roamed over the secluded green cove surrounded by mountain peaks. No photo truly did this place justice.

After several quiet minutes, Cody whispered, "You ready? We have to keep moving if we want to see everything."

Lexi nodded, still not wishing to break the serenity. She trailed Cody back to the Jeep.

They followed the road around the lake, leaving the south shore in the rearview mirror. Lexi admired the many views, noting cabins discreetly tucked into the forest and along the edge of the lake. "Seems to me more people live on the California side."

"I think you're right." Cody gazed over the horizon. "Tell me how you became so knowledgeable about Lake Tahoe."

"My grandparents moved up here when I was eleven, so when they were researching the area—geek that I was—I jumped right in to help."

"Geek?"

"I was very studious. Grades were of the utmost importance to my parents."

"I thought acting was."

Lexi shrugged, that old familiar cloud of failure settling over her. "It was—everything was. They wanted a well-rounded child. Smart, talented, beautiful, witty."

"The Stepford child."

"Exactly. Anyway, back to Gram and Gramps. They fell in love with the Tahoe area, and so did I. I know lots of useless facts, like it's the country's largest alpine lake, and the water is crystal clear, cleaner than the drinking water in most U.S. cities."

୧

Cody laughed at Lexi's dramatic rendition of her knowledge of Lake Tahoe, grateful he'd decided to wait to talk about this morning's fire. Otherwise they wouldn't be having such a lighthearted time. He'd determined to wait until after they shared a nice lunch on the bank of the Truckee River. Then they'd have the drive home to process and strategize.

"Lake Tahoe 'must surely be the fairest picture the whole earth affords.'" He glanced in Lexi's direction. "But I'd say you are."

She smiled. "Mark Twain. Very impressive."

"And very true. Every morning I fall in love with this place all over again." He shook his head. "Sounds cheesy, doesn't it?"

"Not at all. Sounds like you're a man with some connection to his own feelings. A rarity in my world." He heard admiration in her tone.

"It's the perfect place to live. I'm an avid outdoorsman. I like it all—sailing, swimming, sailboarding, parasailing, water skiing, jet skiing, rafting, fishing, snowmobiling, downhill skiing, even an occasional sleigh ride. And let's not forget golf. Sometimes Alph and I drive up to Incline Village for a game. It's a championship course and well worth the drive. You should see it—set on the side of the mountain overlooking the lake. Doesn't get much better."

"Golf with a view."

"Golf with a view—an incredible view. Probably only matched by the area around Heavenly. Those views are gorgeous, too." As they passed Meeks Bay, Cody continued. "This is considered the beginning of the north shore. If you look closely, you'll spot some strategically placed mansions hidden among the trees. Probably less ostentatious than those in Southern California. Up here they have a more rustic look, many built with native wood and stone, but they are mansions nonetheless. Did you know they filmed *The Godfather II* at Ehrman Mansion at Sugar Pine Point State Park?"

"I didn't. I was just thinking what an eclectic place Lake Tahoe is—from the tiniest of cabins to mansions. From the casinos on the south shore to the sleepy villages dotting the west side."

"You're right. And now, mademoiselle, we are approaching Tahoe City—the birthplace of the Truckee River. I thought we'd hit a deli and enjoy lunch on its banks."

"A picnic! How quaint!" Her voice held exuberance, but he

wasn't sure what she was thinking.

"You don't like picnics?"

"Oh no, I'm fond of picnics, but I haven't enjoyed one in years. Probably since I was eleven." She laughed.

"Everything happened when you were eleven." Cody slowed for a pedestrian.

"Pretty much. I'd started getting serious about God, and my parents resented my grandparents' influence over that area of my life. They decided I spent way too much time with those 'religious Holy Rollers'—their terminology, not mine—so they limited me to two weeks every summer rather than the whole break. The first year their edict was in force, I cried almost the entire two and a half months. I was home alone every day with the maid." Lexi's voice cracked. "I was a pretty lonely kid, and my best memories were spending three months a year with my grandparents. It worked well for my parents, too. They traveled extensively and didn't have to mess with a snot-nosed kid."

"I'm sorry." Her stories made him even more hesitant to share his life with her. His was the kind every kid should have but many didn't.

"Wow, talk about a downer. I'm the one who is sorry. You should have been a shrink. I have no problem opening up to you—and for me, that's big."

Cody pulled into the Tahoe House. "Glad to be of assistance. I'll send you my bill." He winked. "You ready for lunch?"

"Sure."

"Everything here is fresh—made right on the premises—and really good. They've got soups, salads, sandwiches, and to-die-for pastries. Since your grandmother wants to put meat on those bones, this is just the place to help with that endeavor."

Lexi shook her head. "Gram would turn me into a roly-poly if I'd let her."

They stopped a moment to study the menu. Once Lexi decided, he stepped up to the counter. "I'd like a roast beef on squaw bread, and she'd like the half sandwich—a veggie—and spinach salad combo. Would you throw in a chocolate truffle turtle torte and two large iced teas?"

"A torte?" Lexi raised her brow.

"Hey, just following your grandmother's orders. Besides, it's worth wasting some calories on." He winked. "I promise."

Once they were back in the Jeep with their lunch, Cody followed Highway 89 north. "This highway is now taking us away from the lake, but the river runs right alongside us and is in view much of the way. There's a nice spot up by the Alpine Meadows turnoff where we can eat right next to the river. Then we'll go up to Squaw Valley where the 1960 Winter Olympics were held. Finally, we'll retrace our path back down to Highway 28 and finish our trek around the lake."

"Sounds good. Maybe sometime we can take a rafting trip." She pointed at many bright blue and yellow inflatable rafts floating on the Truckee.

"Looks so peaceful, doesn't it?"

Cody pulled off the road. He and Lexi carried a big blanket, the ice chest Essie had insisted they bring, and the bag filled with their lunch down to the edge of the river.

Lexi spread out the blanket and plopped down on one side. "This, my friend, is the life." She sighed with contentment and lay back. "The sun feels warm and welcoming." She closed her eyes against its brightness.

Cody dreaded ruining this perfect day. She was more relaxed than he'd ever seen her. His news would shatter that for sure.

They ate in silence, enjoying the sights and sounds of nature and watching groups of rafters float by.

꙳

Once they finished lunch and stowed their garbage in the bag, Cody asked, "So where'd you guys walk today?"

"Just through the neighborhood." Lexi breathed deep, enjoying the fresh air filled with the scents of pine and water. "I can't believe I found this boring as a kid. It's all so—breathtaking."

"That it is." Cody nodded. "So did you guys stay together the whole time?"

"Huh?" Lexi had only been half listening. "What guys?" She crinkled her nose. Was he asking about her and Jamison?

"You and your gram. Were you with her the whole walk?"

Lexi's stomach knotted. "Was there another fire?" She searched Cody's face for the answer, but in her heart, she already knew.

He nodded.

"I have never gone anywhere alone, Cody. Just as you requested."

"One of your grandparents' neighbors claimed she saw a woman fitting your description out walking alone this morning."

She wondered if he now doubted her innocence. "Cody, Gram will tell you that I never left her side." Her tone rang defensive.

He grabbed her hand and gave a squeeze. "I believe you, Lex." He must have seen uncertainty on her face. "I do." He said the words with firm conviction. "I should have waited to bring this up—let you enjoy the rest of the day."

"No. You should have told me before we ever left the house. I had a right to know." The bright blue of the sky and the green landscape no longer captivated her. The world, for her, had just turned a bleak shade of gray.

Cody sucked in a deep breath. "I'm sorry. I just wanted to get you away from your grandparents so we could talk in private. I figured the last half of the drive will give you time to process."

Lexi leaned her head back, releasing a long sigh. "How can this be happening again?"

"There's got to be an explanation. We'll find it—whatever it is."

Lexi resituated herself in a cross-legged position, her head hanging low. *I'm afraid.*

"Essie never even stepped away for a second? Maybe to admire a flower, watch a raccoon, or attempt to follow a squirrel?"

"I can tell you've had many a walk with Gram. She does every one of those things, but I don't recall her ever leaving my side. I'm trying to get her to keep walking, so she no longer has time to linger. I try to get my heart rate up at least a little. When she's with me, we don't dawdle. No more nature walks for her."

Cody nodded. "I do understand why during that first grass fire people remembered seeing you. You were out every day hiking somewhere, but if you haven't been alone, why would someone say you were?"

"Maybe it's somebody who looks like me." Lexi stretched her neck—her shoulders suddenly tight with knots.

"Realistically, how many women do you know who are blond with long golden curls and nearly six feet tall?" Cody eyed her.

"Realistically, I know quite a few." She now tilted her head to the side, stretching it down toward her shoulder.

"I guess you would in your line of work. But I've lived in these mountains five years and have never met, or even seen, another woman who fits your description." He paused. "What. . ." He hesitated, seemingly uncomfortable about his line of thinking.

"About an ex?" she finished for him, not wanting to remember any of them. But she ran through the list in her head.

"Did any of them want something you weren't willing to give?"

She thought hard, but nothing came to mind.

Cody cleared his throat. "What about wives or girlfriends who want you to pay?"

Lexi hung her head. She'd never told Cody that she slept with married men, yet he instinctively knew. Shame flowed through her veins, touching every cell of her being. How low she'd fallen.

"Lexi, you've repented. God's forgiven you."

She raised her tear-streaked face and looked him in the eye. "How can He forgive such an atrocity?"

"Because He does, Lexi. Because He does." Cody's face held no judgment or condemnation. It made it easier to believe God didn't, either.

"King David, the man after God's own heart, not only slept with a married woman, but he had her husband killed."

Lexi sniffed. "I haven't done that." How was it he always knew the right thing to say? She looked at him through blurry, tear-filled eyes and decided he was the most attractive man she'd ever met. Someday some girl would be lucky—mighty lucky indeed.

"There are a lot of people who might hate me for one reason or another, and rightly so. Are you thinking this is some sort of revenge?"

Cody shrugged again and shook his head. "I don't know. Nothing else makes sense."

"Maybe I deserve whatever happens to me, even if I had nothing to do with the fires."

"Lexi, we all deserve God's wrath, but He doesn't work that way. He is merciful and gracious to us."

Her much-regretted past, her present reality, the possibility of being punished for a crime she didn't commit, and the loving God who was calling her back to Himself all blended together in this moment in time. Lexi was overcome with more emotions than she knew how to deal with. She tried to hold back, but one sob escaped, and before she could reinforce the dam and hold her tears at bay, the onslaught broke through any restraint, and Lexi wept.

Cody pulled her into his arms, knocking her cap off in the process. He held her against his chest, running his hand over her hair. "It will be okay, Lexi. I promise that somehow it will be okay." He said the words over and over, and she knew that he'd do everything in his power to make it so.

She rested her head against his heart, hearing the steady, calming beat. The last arms she'd cried in had been her gramps's when she was still a little girl. In the circle of Cody's muscular arms, Lexi felt safe. For the first time since childhood, having a man's arms hold her felt good and right. How strange. She'd never before wanted a man to hold her, but she never wanted this man to let her go.

❦

Cody didn't rush her. He knew he'd hold her forever if he could. While she cried, he prayed, asking God to provide answers. When the sobs subsided, he kept her close, waiting patiently until she was ready to pull away. When she finally did, his arms ached with the emptiness. She rose, and they packed up their picnic, neither saying a word.

Once inside the Jeep, Cody drove Lexi to the Olympic site, but he wasn't sure she even noticed. When they arrived back in Tahoe City, he turned left and finished the drive around the north shore. When they hit Incline Village, the upscale community built on the side of some fairly steep mountains, Cody commented, "This is where we golf occasionally."

She nodded but didn't comment.

Leaving Incline Village was his favorite part of the drive, because the route often ran right next to the water's edge. The views of the lake were much better on this side. Nevertheless, he didn't bother pointing out anything else. Lexi was too deep in her own thoughts. He doubted she even saw a thing.

When Cody pulled onto their street, he saw a strange car in front of Alph and Essie's house. He opted to bypass their driveway for his own.

"Lexi?"

She turned and faced him.

"Your grandparents have company. Do you want to freshen up at my place before going home?"

She nodded, checking out the Buick in her grandparents' drive as she headed toward Cody's front door. "I don't recognize that car, do you?"

"Nope."

Cody fetched Lexi a fresh hand towel and washcloth and showed her to his guest bathroom. "Sorry, but I don't have any face soap. Guys don't have special bars for different body parts."

"Thanks. I'll make do."

While Lexi washed away the traces of a broken heart, Cody went out front to unload their picnic items from the car. A woman stood at the bottom of Alph and Essie's porch.

He heard her yell, "If you won't do anything about your granddaughter, then I'm sure the police will!"

Cody rushed across the street. "Everything all right over here?" He searched each face for a clue.

"Sybil says she saw Lexi set a fire this morning near her cabin, but I told her Lexi was with me all morning, making her accusation impossible." Gram raised her chin, emphasizing the rightness of her words.

Lexi couldn't have picked a worse possible moment to join them. When Cody saw her coming, he wished for a way to head her off.

When Sybil spotted her, she pointed. "That's her. I knew it was her." She faced Lexi. "If I see you out again, I'll call the police. Don't come near my street!" With that demand, she climbed in her car and sped off.

six

"That woman is nuttier than a fruitcake," Gram informed them as Sybil drove away. "I mean, I stood here and told her you were with me the whole morning until you left with Cody. She all but called me a liar. And I thought Sybil Green was my friend." Gram turned in a huff and marched into the house.

Gramps followed her. "Can't trust anybody these days. There was a time when folks watched out for one another. Not anymore." He paused in the doorway. "You two coming?"

"Be there in a minute, Alph," Cody hollered and turned to Lexi. "You holding up?"

She nodded. *You precious, precious man. I never thought I'd feel anything positive about your gender—not ever. But you've sneaked into the back door of my heart.*

"What are you thinking?"

That you are a more wonderful friend than I deserve. She shrugged, unwilling to voice her thoughts.

"Are you ready to tell your grandparents what's going on?"

"Not yet. I won't leave the house anymore unless you're with me. We'll drive miles from here to hike."

"Lexi, if this is some kind of revenge, none of those things will stop whoever it is." His gaze was tender and sweet like warm, melted chocolate. "Besides, you'll be miserable under house arrest."

"Not as miserable as I'd be in jail." She laughed, but the sound was hollow and meaningless.

"So you're willing to become a prisoner here, in hopes of stopping the problem?"

She nodded. "If I tell my grandparents, they'll be upset. My grandpa's heart has never fully recovered from his last heart attack. I can't risk what this burden might do to him."

Lexi knew Cody didn't agree with her line of thinking, but he accepted it without trying to push his own agenda.

"All right, Lexi, but I'm counting on you to keep your promise and stay inside. You're just lucky the press lost interest in the grass fire story and let it die. But all that said, don't you think your grandparents will notice the change in your pattern if you suddenly stick close to home?"

"You're right. As always, I think I'm protecting them by being less than honest. Will you come with me to tell them?"

Cody nodded.

She'd never felt so needy and vulnerable. He must have sensed it, because he pulled her into his arms, wrapping her tight against his chest. "I'm walking through this with you, Lexi," he spoke into her hair. "No matter what happens, no matter how long it takes, I'll be right beside you. And so will God."

"Thank you." She closed her eyes and rested her head against his shoulder. His words gave her the courage she needed to get through this. They stood together in her grandparents' front yard for several minutes. She may have stayed longer, if he'd let her. He kissed her head and released his hold, grabbing her hand and pulling her forward. Just before opening the front door, he paused and turned toward her, placing a hand on each side of her face. Their gazes magnetized, drawing them ever closer.

Lexi's heart beat out its own song against her ribs. She anticipated his lips meeting her own. Never had she wanted a man's kiss more.

He stopped short, resting his forehead against hers. "God loves you, Lexi. Get the idea out of your head that He's trying to punish you through this. The world is full of mean and evil people who affect innocent lives."

"I'm not so innocent, Cody."

" 'Cleanse me with hyssop, and I will be clean; wash me, and I will be whiter than snow.' Lexi, He did that for you. You asked for forgiveness, and He washed you whiter than snow. Like any of us, confessing doesn't erase every consequence, but it frees us from guilt, shame, and condemnation."

He closed his eyes. "Father, enable Lexi to understand forgiveness and all that it brings. May she refuse to give in to the shame and self-condemnation. In Jesus' name, amen."

He hugged her tight for one brief moment and led her through her grandparents' front door. Then he released her hand.

Lexi swallowed hard. "I'll be right back." She moved down the hall and into her bathroom. Bright eyes and flushed cheeks reflected in the mirror. She splashed her face with cool water.

"What a good reminder of how ill-suited you and Cody would be," she whispered. "While he has God on his mind, you have kissing on yours." *What in the world is wrong with me? It's been years since I've wanted to be kissed.*

When Lexi returned from the restroom, Cody and her grandparents were sitting on the deck enjoying iced tea. A frosty glass awaited her. She took the empty seat at the table with Cody on her left, Gram on her right, and Gramps across from her. She took her time squeezing her lemon slice, not sure how to broach the subject that needed discussing. Cody and Gram were conversing about some new wood chipper that was out on the market.

Finally Cody cleared his throat. "I think Lexi wanted to tell the two of you something."

At his prompt, Lexi spilled the whole fire story.

"So Sybil Green is only one of many eyewitnesses who claim to have seen Lexi near the vicinity of a fire," Cody said, summing up her paragraphs of explanation into one sentence packaged with clarity.

Lexi would never forget the horror that settled on Gram's face. Or the fear. Gram sat in stunned silence while Cody explained his theory, at least with the first fire.

As the shock wore off, Gram's spunky personality kicked into gear. She hit her fist on the table with determination. "We'll have none of this. Lexi is innocent, and she won't hide out like some criminal. We will walk tomorrow morning and every morning that follows." She rose. "And that matter is settled," she stated, leaving the deck and going inside.

The following morning, Gram came into Lexi's room and threw the covers back. "Time for our walk. What are you still doing in bed?" She pulled the curtains back. "Rise and shine, sleepyhead."

"I'm not going." Lexi pulled the covers back up and over her head.

"You are going." Determination laced through Gram's words.

Lexi sat up. "I need to spend some extra time with the Lord today. How about if you go without me, at least until I pray this through."

Gram nodded. "I will this time." Lexi knew her unspoken thought was, *But I'll not put up with this for long.*

Gram left the house alone. Lexi went and poured herself some coffee and grabbed her Bible and journal. At Cody's suggestion, she'd decided to record her journey back home to God.

Lexi felt a good cry coming and decided to get dressed and sit on the private porch off her bedroom. She wanted to cry in private and couldn't bear the thought of being cooped up inside on such a beautiful day.

She slipped into a pair of jeans and a T-shirt and sank onto the chaise lounge. "Lord, show me what to do. I have no idea."

Her cell phone rang. It was Cody. "Hi."

"Lexi, where are you?" She knew by the frustration in his voice that there had been another fire.

"I'm on the deck outside my bedroom."

"Alone?"

"Yes."

He let out a sigh. "What happened to not leaving the house?"

"Cody, I'm two feet from it." Her heart was pounding. "Where did it happen this time?"

"Two streets over. Not only do they have an eyewitness, but she named you as the arsonist."

Lexi closed her eyes. *God, where are You?* "She's saying she saw Lexi Eastridge set the fire?"

"Not Lexi Eastridge, but the Newcombs' granddaughter. Get inside the house, and please go sit in the same room with your grandfather. I'll be there as soon as I can."

Lexi did as he asked. Her mouth had gone dry. *God, where are You?* She swallowed against the lump lodged in her throat. *I need You.* She went and sat on the couch in the family room. Gramps was in his chair with commentaries and several versions of the Bible spread on the two end tables placed at the sides of his recliner.

"What's up, Lexi girl?"

She burst into tears. "Another fire—this morning. Someone is saying she saw me light it. Not someone who looks like me, but me."

"That's nuts." Gramps laid his glasses and book aside. "You've been here the whole time."

"I know that. You know that. But how can we prove it?"

"Why should we have to prove it?" His brows drew together. "What happened to innocent until proven guilty?"

"I guess an eyewitness pretty much rules out innocence and establishes guilt."

Gramps drew his mouth together in a hard, firm line.

The doorbell ringing caused both Lexi and Gramps to jump. She glanced at him and saw her own fear reflected in his eyes. He rose from his recliner, and she stood to follow, heart pounding like a tom-tom.

"You wait here, Lexi girl."

She returned to the couch. "God, please help me." She strained to hear, but only a muffle of men's voices came to her. Then she heard footsteps on the wood floor—several sets, drawing closer and closer. She closed her eyes and sucked in a deep breath.

"Lexi." Gramps cleared his throat. His face was ashen. Two policemen stood behind him.

"These gentlemen have a few questions they'd like to ask you." Gramps returned to his recliner, and he motioned for the men to have a seat, but they didn't.

Both stood, watching Lexi with intense eyes—one pair blue and one brown.

"I'm Sergeant Christopher, and this is Officer Elliott. Can you give us your name?"

"Alexandria Eastridge." Lexi's voice quivered.

"We have received several reports that link you with the recent acts of arson." Officer Elliott proceeded to read Lexi her Miranda rights. "Do you want an attorney present?"

Lexi's thoughts whirled. She couldn't think clearly. Three

pairs of eyes rested on her, waiting for a response. "I don't think so."

"Fine, then we'll proceed. Where were you this morning, ma'am, between five and seven?"

The front door slammed. Gram stormed in from her walk. "What's going on?" She placed her hands on her hips.

"Everything is all right, Essie. Why don't you have a seat?"

"Ma'am, for the record, will you state your name and relationship to Ms. Eastridge?" The sergeant spoke in a no-nonsense tone.

"I'm Essie Newcomb, her grandmother." Then she settled on the couch next to Lexi and leaned forward slightly as if to shield her from these men.

"Ma'am"—they'd refocused their attention on Lexi—"you may proceed."

"Between five and seven, I was here. I haven't left the house at all today."

"We can testify to that being the truth." Gram leaned forward, eager to help.

"No disrespect, ma'am, but you only just arrived"—the sergeant glanced at his watch—"what, four minutes ago?"

Little did they know Gram didn't give up without a good fight. The woman had the tenacity of a bulldog. "But she was in bed when I left."

"What time did you leave the house?"

"Somewhere between six thirty and six forty-five."

"Did you actually see her with your own eyes or just assume she was in her room?"

"I saw her. I went in and woke her up. We had a conversation." They didn't intimidate Gram.

"And then you left the house?"

She nodded.

"And didn't return until. . ." Again he checked the time. "Six minutes ago?"

"That's correct, but I know she didn't leave."

"How do you know that, ma'am, if you weren't in the home as an eyewitness?"

Gram continued to tell the whole story, and Lexi cringed at how incriminating the facts seemed.

Both policemen kept stoic expressions that Lexi couldn't read, so she had no idea what they must be thinking.

"Sir, were you here in the home all morning?"

Gramps nodded.

"Will you speak your answer, please?"

"Yes, I was here all morning. I awoke around five and haven't left the premises."

"Did you have visual contact with your granddaughter this morning?" The sergeant studied Gramps over the top of his reading glasses.

"Yes, sir, I did. I saw her come in and get a cup of coffee right after Essie—my wife—left on her walk. Then she returned to her room, and I heard her stirring about, probably getting gussied up for the day. You know how women do."

"So though you couldn't see her, you could hear her the entire time?"

"Not the entire time. But often enough to indicate there was life in the house."

The sergeant puckered his lips and made more notations on his report.

"Ms. Eastridge, can you tell me what you did this morning and the approximate time you did it? Start at six."

Lexi figured since Gram already told everything, she'd follow suit. "I woke up around five but didn't want to face the day, so I pulled the covers over my head but never quite fell back asleep." She then proceeded to share the rest of the morning, even Cody's phone call.

❧

Cody finally found someone to cover the rest of his shift. He hopped in his Jeep and drove to Alph and Essie's. A million emotions surged through him, but the overriding two were frustration and fear. He wished Lexi had a better alibi for the morning. He'd called his dad earlier, but he was in a meeting. As the police chief in Reno, he would help guide them through this mess.

Turning onto their street, he spotted the police car sitting in front of their house. His stomach knotted. He pulled his phone from the front pocket of his uniform shirt. Staring at the silent cell phone, he said, "Dad, I really need you to call me back."

Cody rang the front doorbell. He figured just walking in might be inappropriate at this point in time.

A few moments later, Alph answered. Concern lined his face. He led Cody into the family room.

His eyes met Lexi's. They were wide and filled with anxiety. She was in the corner of the couch, and he'd never seen her looking more vulnerable. He wanted more than anything to take her in his arms and hold her until all this misunderstanding passed by.

seven

"Cooper, you need something? You're disrupting a police investigation." Elliott reminded Cody of a cocky rooster, the way he stuck out his chest and strutted like he was the most important person on the planet.

"I'm a neighbor and live across the street. Just checking on things. Everybody okay?"

Essie resembled an old bear whose cub faced danger. Alph was quiet and contemplative, probably locked into a prayer conversation with God, which was his way. Lexi—ah, sweet Lexi. How he wished he could spare her this, but all he could do was walk through it beside her.

"We'd like to finish up here, if you don't mind." Elliott glared at him.

"Be my guest." Cody folded his arms across his chest and leaned against a bar stool. His stance appeared casual enough, but inside was a lion ready to pounce should they make one wrong move.

"This is a private matter," Sarge informed Cody.

"This is our home, and he's welcome to stay." Alph spoke in a subdued tone but with a firm deliverance.

"Have it your way." Elliott focused all his attention on Lexi. "You're our number one suspect, and we'll be watching you. We have more interviews to conduct, but don't think about leaving town." The officer reminded Cody of Barney Fife from *The Andy Griffith Show*.

"You can't possibly expect her to stay in Stateline while the investigation proceeds," said Cody.

Elliott glanced at the sergeant. "Well, for sure don't leave the state until this is resolved. Are you clear on that?"

"Yes." Her face was pale and her eyes huge.

"That'll be all then. We'll show ourselves out."

As soon as the front door shut, Cody said, "Lexi, get ready. We're going to Reno to see my dad."

She glanced at her grandparents.

"Alph, you and Essie are welcome, too."

"Not me." Alph rubbed his knee. "These old bones hate making that trip anymore."

"Essie?"

Cody knew she wanted to. She glanced from him to Alph and then to Lexi. Finally she shook her head. "I think I'll pass."

"You sure?"

She nodded. "You two run along."

Cody's cell beeped. "Finally. It's my dad. Will you excuse me?" He walked out the back door and onto the deck.

After filling in his dad on the situation, they set up a time to meet for lunch. While Lexi got ready, he ran to the firehouse and grabbed copies of the reports they had regarding the three grass fires.

He and Lexi arrived at Bertha Miranda's Mexican Restaurant & Cantina a little early. "My family used to come here every Sunday after church during my growing-up years. People stand in line early just so they don't have to wait for a seat later." He opened her car door.

"You have a lot of nice family memories, don't you?" Some of Lexi's color had returned.

He held open the heavy wooden door for her to enter. "I do. I have a nice family. I look forward to you meeting them sometime."

"Me, too," Lexi responded.

Cody's expression was warm and his eyes tender. Just the way he gazed at her made her feel special—even if they were only friends.

"May I help you?" a proper Hispanic gentleman asked.

"Table for three. A booth if you have it." They had arrived a little after the typical lunch crowd, so the place was no longer jam-packed.

The tall, thin man led them to a booth.

Cody pointed at a portrait as they trailed behind the older man. "That's Bertha Miranda," he whispered.

Lexi slid onto the vinyl-covered seat, and Cody slipped in next to her. His closeness wreaked havoc with her senses. Sometimes she longed to lay her head on his shoulder or have him hold her again.

A nice-looking man with graying sideburns slipped into the seat directly across from them. "Son, it's good to see you. And you must be Lexi." He offered his right hand.

"Lexi, this is my dad, Police Chief Frank Cooper. Dad, this is Alexandria Eastridge, aka Lexi."

They greeted one another. Lexi couldn't help but think that the son would be just as distinguished looking one day as his father was today. *He'll make some lucky girl a fine catch—a fine catch indeed.*

"So, Lexi, is there anybody that you can think of who hates you enough to try and malign your reputation, possibly even pave the way to a jail sentence?"

He said "jail sentence" so calmly, so matter-of-factly, but those same words made her want to cry out in terror. "Not that I can think of."

Their waiter came with water and then took their orders. Lexi wasn't hungry but ordered some soup just to be polite.

"Nobody, huh? Possibly another model whom you replaced?"

Lexi thought, but no one came to mind.

Chief Cooper rattled off an entire list of possibilities, but none of them jibed with Lexi.

"I just can't imagine anyone doing this to me or anybody else." She shook her head.

"Sadly, I see this sort of thing all the time. Revenge sounds sweet, though I don't think in reality it ever is." Chief Cooper looked over the notes Cody handed him.

"Here's what I'm thinking: You spend the next few days with a constant companion. Go nowhere without this person, not even the bathroom. Then if your nemesis strikes, everyone will know it's a hate crime."

Lexi didn't say anything, but for an introvert like her, the idea of someone being glued to her hip sounded daunting. *But better than jail.*

"I want you to start making lists of every person you perturbed in any way. Cover every event from junior high on. Based on my experience, I'm certain someone wants revenge. I've seen it too many times, and the pattern is always the same."

"So can they arrest her at this point?" Cody questioned.

Chief Cooper shrugged and leaned out of the way while the waiter set a steaming plate of enchiladas in front of him. "Depends on how confident the DA is that he can make the charges stick. I know the sheriff of Douglas County pretty well. I did him a favor a few years back. Let's head over to Stateline after lunch and meet with him."

Cody bit into one of his ground beef tacos. "That would be great, Dad. Thanks." He smiled at Lexi and squeezed her hand under the table.

Lexi dipped a spoon into the tortilla soup. This whole

ordeal felt surreal. "Thank you, sir."

To think several weeks ago she'd perceived Cody as an enemy. Now he'd become her hero and her friend. How grateful she felt to him and his dad.

❧

After lunch Cody held his Jeep door open for Lexi. She'd been quiet through their meal, only speaking when spoken to. The stress of this ordeal was taking its toll.

He longed to draw her into his arms and hold her, reassure her, but he stood back while she climbed in. When she was settled in his passenger seat, he ached to kiss her and promise her this would all be okay. But would it? He wished he knew. God seemed slow in answering prayers where Lexi was concerned.

He shut her door, making his way around to the driver's side of the vehicle. He paused before turning the key, searching for words of wisdom or encouragement, but none came.

Finally he turned the ignition, and the engine growled to life. Shifting into reverse, they started the trek back to Stateline.

"We should have had my dad come to us. Guess I wasn't thinking."

His hand rested on the gearshift knob, and she laid hers on top of his. "Thank you—for everything."

He turned his hand over, and hers slipped into his like it belonged there. "You're welcome."

They drove in silence with his hand holding hers and his heart wanting so much more.

When they pulled into the parking lot of the sheriff's office, his dad rolled in right behind them. Cody and Lexi each took a chair in the waiting area while his dad spoke to a woman at the desk. Moments later the sheriff stepped out from behind a closed door. Cody recognized him from his election poster. He held out his right hand, a grin splitting his chubby face. "Frank Cooper!" They shook hands. "Come on back to my office." He motioned with his head toward the door he'd just come through. A moment later, both men vanished behind the locked door.

"Why does your dad believe me?" Lexi asked. "I mean, he doesn't even know me. For that matter, why are you so sure I'm innocent?"

"The Lord. Discernment. Your character. I'm not sure how I know, but without a doubt, I do."

"Cody, Lexi." His dad stood holding the door open, motioning for them to follow. They both jumped up. Cody paused for Lexi to go first. When her gaze met his, fear radiated from her large blue eyes. He smiled, hoping to reassure her.

"George Howard, this is Alexandria Eastridge."

He held out his right hand and shook Lexi's. Cody noted the recognition in the sheriff's eyes. He must have seen one of her commercials.

"And this is my son, Cody Cooper. He's a firefighter down at three in Zephyr Cove."

"Cody." The man had a firm grip as he shook Cody's hand. "Have a seat, everyone."

Sheriff Howard settled in a chair on his side of the desk.

"Chief Cooper has filled me in on the fact that you're a celebrity. I'd only heard that you were somebody's granddaughter. I agree with the chief; this is probably some type of revenge or hate crime."

❧

Lexi closed her eyes, a tiny ray of hope illuminating her situation. "Thank you." The words were a mere whisper.

"Because of Chief Cooper and his position in our state, we

will grant you a privilege not afforded to just anyone."

Lexi nodded. *Another rescue by the Cooper family.*

"Based on our assessment of the situation and the sheriff's wise advice, we are encouraging you to come back to Reno with my wife and me for a few days." Chief Cooper glanced from her to Cody. "We'll see if the fires continue in your absence."

Lexi didn't want to leave her grandparents' place to stay with perfect strangers. She glanced at Cody. He reached for her hand and gave it a reassuring squeeze.

"Maybe Cody can smuggle you out in the middle of the night so no one sees you leaving."

"I'm headed to Reno for the weekend anyway." Cody turned his gaze on her. "My brother is getting married this weekend. You can go as my plus one."

"Great idea." Chief Cooper rose and shook the sheriff's hand. "Thanks for working with us on this. Call me when the next fire happens, or I'll call you when we're smuggling her back up the mountain."

"Sounds good." The sheriff shook each of their hands. "We'll do what we can on this end."

Cody ushered Lexi out the door with a guiding hand on her back. They stopped in the lobby. "Bring her down about three or four, and Lexi, I'd lay across the backseat until you turn toward Carson City on Highway 50. We don't want anyone other than your grandparents aware of this. They need to be discreet. If anyone asks, you're home with the flu."

Lexi nodded.

Chief Cooper gave Cody a hug. "See you tomorrow then. Your mom will have the guest room ready for Lexi. Just show her to it whenever you arrive. We probably won't be up to greet you."

"Sure. We'll see you later in the morning."

Chief Cooper took Lexi's right hand and held it between his hands. "It was good to meet you, Lexi. I'm sorry it has to be under these circumstances, but I'm glad you'll be joining us for Brady and Kendall's wedding. Sleep as late as you like tomorrow, and we'll have a pot of coffee on when you wake up."

"Thank you—for everything."

"My pleasure."

All three exited the building. Cody opened the passenger door of his Jeep and waited while Lexi climbed in and got settled.

Her mind was reeling. What had become a permanent knot resided in her stomach. She just wanted to return to LA, but now she wasn't allowed to leave Nevada. This all felt surreal—Oz-like—as if she'd tripped and fallen into someone else's life.

Cody opening her door surprised her, and she jumped. She'd not realized they'd arrived back at her grandparents'.

As she slid out of the Jeep, Cody pulled her into his arms. He hugged her tight, saying nothing—just holding her.

Lexi wanted to relax in his embrace and give herself over to his affections. But she was much too fragile to handle his tenderness without falling apart, so she remained stiff in his embrace, stepping out of it as soon as he loosened his hold.

She saw the hurt and confusion written across his face. He'd only offered the solace of a friend, and she'd rejected it.

"I just need to get this over with."

He nodded and placed his hand across her back, propelling her forward.

&

Cody longed to comfort Lexi, but when he'd tried, she'd remained cold and distant. The strain of all this was showing on her face.

He followed her inside, and she settled on the end of the couch, closest to her grandfather's chair. Cody sat on the other end.

"I need to talk to you guys."

Alph picked up the remote and clicked the television off.

Lexi filled them in on all that had transpired.

Essie folded down the footrest on her recliner with force and jumped up out of her chair. "This is not right! You shouldn't have to leave when you haven't done anything." She got teary. "You've only been here a month and promised me the spring and maybe even summer."

Lexi rose and hugged her grandmother. "I'll be back." Her voice cracked with fresh emotion.

"I've heard that before."

Lexi glanced at Cody, as if to say, "What do I do now?"

Cody, too, rose and joined the huddle, taking Essie by the upper arms and turning her to face him. "This isn't Lexi's fault. Do you think she wants to leave you and stay with my family? No, she doesn't, but we are trying to keep her safe. Will you let my dad and me do that?"

Essie sucked in a deep breath. She pulled her lips together in a tight line, and Cody spotted the tears pooling in her eyes. She nodded her head. Cody pulled her into his arms. He'd grown to love her like his own grandmother.

She hugged Cody back—a much better hug than he'd gotten from Lexi. He heard a sniffle, and her body quivered. "It'll be all right."

She pulled back and gazed into his eyes, nodding her tear-streaked face. Then she grabbed Lexi's hand. "You do whatever you have to do. Gramps and I will be here waiting for you to come back." Then her tears fell harder, faster. "Excuse me." She pulled loose from Cody's light hold and left the room.

Lexi wiped at her eyes. "This is about more than me leaving now, isn't it? It's about all the years I never came." She turned toward her grandfather. "It's about the years of neglect."

He nodded.

"I'm sorry, Gramps. So very sorry. It wasn't because I didn't want to be here. I never wanted to hurt you."

She went to his chair and hugged him for several minutes.

"I love you, my Lexi girl." Even Alph's eyes seemed a little shiny to Cody. "And I forgive you. Why don't you go tell your gram what you just told me?"

"I will."

۶

Cody gave Lexi an encouraging smile as she passed him on her way to Gram's bedroom. She longed to cash in on the hug he'd offered earlier, but she didn't let herself. Whenever Cody's chocolate eyes rested on her, her heart melted in response.

Lexi found Gram in her bathroom, reapplying her powder. "May I come in?"

Gram nodded her head.

"Just now, those tears were about more than me leaving, weren't they?" Lexi settled on the edge of the tub.

Gram made eye contact through the mirror. "I'm hurt that you stayed away so long." Gram blinked fast and furious.

Lexi hung her head, fighting her own tears. How much did she dare say?

She raised her gaze back to the mirror. "I'm sorry. I honestly never meant to hurt or abandon either of you."

Gram turned to face her. "I know that, but you did. We got the token Sunday phone call, but you never had time for us. Your friends and your life in LA were obviously more important than your relationship with us."

"Gram, that's not true." Lexi rose, and mere inches separated them.

"A picture is worth a thousand words. And the picture you painted was that we weren't worth the effort."

Lexi felt like a waterfall rolled over her cheeks from the river of her eyes. "I do understand why you would make that assumption, but there was no place I wanted to be more than here. I just couldn't face you."

Gram wrapped Lexi in her embrace. "What in the world are you talking about—you couldn't face us?"

Without being too graphic, Lexi became real with her grandmother. She shared pieces of her life story, bits of her shame, and boatloads of her personal sorrow. They cried together, baptizing the other with their tears. The end result was sweet, bringing healing, forgiveness, and hope for a renewed closeness in the future. Lexi left the bathroom both exhausted and exhilarated.

Cody had long since gone home. Lexi shared a sweet dinner with her grandparents and a tender good-bye scene that evening before they went to bed, promising never to let miles keep them apart for long ever again.

eight

At three in the morning, Cody crept across the street. Darkness blanketed him. The entire neighborhood was black, and no sign of life appeared. He tapped once on the French door leading to her little private patio. She opened it, motioning him inside. Her bed was made, and atop it sat a large duffel bag and a smaller bag.

"Is that it?" he whispered, pointing to the two pieces of luggage.

"I packed light. Those are my grandparents'." He lifted the large tote over his shoulder and picked up the second bag.

Lexi grabbed her large leather purse, which was almost big enough to count as luggage. He paused at the door, holding it open for her. She led the way into the blackness. He locked and shut the door, following close behind Lexi. She climbed into the backseat of his Jeep while he put her luggage into the very back.

Cody started his car and pulled out of the driveway. He followed Highway 50 to Highway 28. A few minutes later, he announced to Lexi that they'd turned off toward Reno. She sat up.

After a few more minutes, she asked, "Are you sure your parents don't mind me staying there?"

"Not at all. My brother Brady brought home all kinds of strays. I figure it's my turn," he joked, hoping to lighten her mood.

"Strays?"

"Dogs, cats, and kids."

Lexi remained quiet the rest of the ride. Cody had no idea how to ease her anxiety, so he said nothing—just shot up a little prayer for God's peace to permeate.

❧

Cody turned into a neighborhood. The sign said COUGHLIN RANCH. From what Lexi could see, everything was well manicured with grass, flowers, and trees. After a couple of turns, he pulled to a stop at the end of a cul-de-sac. He unloaded her luggage then led her up the sidewalk to the front porch. He laid down her things and fished through the keys on his ring for the right one. Finally he unlocked the door and pushed it open, standing aside for her to enter first. The front door led into a great room. A lamp had been left on, so Lexi could see enough to know Mrs. Cooper had good taste. She liked clean lines without a lot of clutter. The overall effect was warm and welcoming.

Cody led Lexi down the hall, stopping at the second door on the right. He flipped a light switch and laid her things on a chest at the foot of her bed. The bedroom was feminine but not frilly. The brown and pink held great eye appeal.

"The bathroom is across the hall. Knowing my mom, she'll have fresh towels laid out, but I'll double-check." He dashed across the hall. "Yep, you're all taken care of. Do you need anything?"

Lexi shook her head. She'd stopped just inside the door, wishing Cody didn't have to leave, wishing she wasn't in this mess, wishing for a million things that would never happen.

She glanced at Cody. He hovered in the doorway, leaning against the jamb. His eyes reflected her weariness. "Are you driving back home?"

"No. I'll be right down the hall. I'll stay through the

weekend and all the wedding activities." His whiskers shadowed his jaw and chin.

"I don't have to attend all the wedding festivities. I mean, I don't even know the couple. It could be awkward."

"I want you to." When she didn't respond, he asked, "Please? I thought about inviting you anyway but just never did."

Their gazes fused, and Lexi felt the connection. Her heart shifted to the next gear. Cody must have felt it as well. He moved toward her—slow, intentional.

She should turn away, step in the opposite direction, but her feet wouldn't respond. They held her in place as if she had cement in her shoes.

Their gazes never separated. Cody slipped his hand around her neck. His head moved toward her in what felt like slow motion. She swallowed. He placed his other hand on the back of her waist, gently pulling her toward him. She complied, and he wrapped her in his arms, folding her against him in a protective hug. His lips met hers, and Lexi knew for certain, at that exact moment, that she'd fallen deeply in love with Cody Cooper.

The kiss was slow, tender, undemanding. The sweetness of it left her wanting more.

When he lifted his mouth from hers, he didn't loosen his hold. Lexi felt dazed by the wonder of his kiss, and she saw the same emotions swimming in Cody's eyes.

He drank in her face with his eyes, making her feel slightly embarrassed. Would he see the flaws and imperfections?

He lowered his head back to her lips, and Lexi anticipated his touch. He took more time with his second kiss, leaving Lexi feeling light-headed.

"I'd better go." He gently pushed Lexi away from himself.

His abrupt change left Lexi questioning his thoughts. She

ducked her head so he couldn't see her disappointment and turned away from him, wrapping her arms around her waist.

He turned her back around to face him, his hands on her shoulders, keeping her at arm's length. He gently raised her chin until their eyes met, and he returned his hand to her shoulder.

"I don't want to leave, Lexi, but I have to. I'd never use or take advantage of you, and for that not to happen, I have to set firm boundaries for myself."

His words poured over her broken soul like a healing balm.

"I'm on vacation for the wedding, so I'll see you in the morning. . .and the morning after that and the morning after that. I'm not going anywhere."

This man knew how to connect with her heart on every level and leave her speechless at the same time.

He kissed the top of her head. "Sleep tight." He slipped into the dark hall, closing the door as he left.

Lexi fell across the bed, hugging a pillow against her. Yep, no more doubts or uncertainty. She loved Cody. Many delicious emotions swirled around her as she relived the last five minutes over and over. She fell asleep on top of the comforter, still in her clothes but with a smile on her face.

⁂

When Lexi came out into the great room a few hours later, she refused to meet Cody's gaze head-on. He'd barely slept and couldn't wait to see her again. She, however, must be feeling shy or uncertain about the whole incident.

"You hungry?"

"More in need of caffeine." She moved toward the kitchen. "Do you mind if I help myself?"

"Not at all. My parents want you to make yourself at home here." He trailed her to the pot, standing nearby.

"You want a cup?" she asked.

He shook his head. She finished pouring and added some cream. When she turned, she nearly ran into him. He grabbed her cup and steadied it.

"Did you need something?"

He set her cup on the counter and lifted her chin until she finally made eye contact.

"That's better."

A puzzled expression furrowed her brow. Then he kissed her soundly on the mouth. "Just so you know: I'm not a guy who toys with women's emotions, nor am I a guy who kisses every pretty girl I meet. I kissed you last night because you mean something to me."

Lexi stared at the floor. He lifted her chin again. "Caring for someone and sharing affection isn't anything to be embarrassed about."

A tiny smile settled on her mouth. "This is all new to me—not the kissing but the caring."

"So, are you saying you care?" he teased.

"I don't know what I'm saying." She turned to grab her cup.

"Well, here is what I'm saying." He pulled her back around again before she could pick up the mug. "I think you're pretty wonderful."

She smiled. " 'Pretty wonderful.' I like that."

Her smile always caused him to catch his breath. Lexi was in a league of her own. "I wouldn't kiss you unless I thought this thing had places to go."

"What do you mean?" Her brows drew together.

"A future—you and me. I'm way too old for recreational dating and haven't participated in recreational kissing since college."

Lexi looked panicked.

"Don't worry, I'm not asking you to marry me—yet. But

one day, I just might." He handed her the cup she'd poured a few minutes ago. "There is some French toast and bacon warming in the oven. If that sounds too heavy, there's yogurt, granola, or stuff to make a smoothie."

❧

Lexi's head spun. No man had ever considered her marriage material before, and the fact that Cody did touched her heart deeper than he'd ever know. But was she? She'd never let her thoughts go that direction. What did she want from the rest of life, now that the modeling had ended?

"Lexi?"

"Huh?"

"You still here with me?" Cody had stuck his face near hers.

"Yeah, sorry." She carried her coffee over to the bar and perched on a stool. "What were you asking?"

"Breakfast? What's your pleasure?"

Out of habit, Lexi almost passed on food, using coffee to take the edge off her hunger until lunch. But her stomach growled. "I think I'll have the French toast. I'm living wild today. Hey, where are your parents?"

"They are both at work."

"So when will we meet?" The later the better, as far as she was concerned.

"Tomorrow at the wedding. You'll meet the whole fam."

His announcement caused Lexi's stomach to drop. "Do any of them read the tabloids?"

Cody wrapped her in his arms. "Doesn't matter if they do, because you are a new creation in Christ—forgiven, washed anew, and loved." Cody kissed her cheek. "Loved, Lexi—more than you can ever understand." His voice had grown husky, and she was pretty sure he meant by more than just the Lord. The mere thought brought a lump to her throat.

I love you, too. Her heart spilled over with tender feelings and gratitude. Maybe she really was a new person and really did have a new life just around the corner. *But not until tomorrow. Not until all this mess is cleared up.*

❧

Lexi felt gorgeous when she waltzed into the great room the following afternoon. Cody's eyes told her all she needed to know. No one else had to think so, but she wanted him to be proud of her.

He rose and met her. "Whoa, baby, you clean up nice." He took her hand and spun her around like one would during a dance.

He'd really not seen her in much besides hiking boots and T-shirts. Today she took extra care with her hair and makeup, and she'd donned a gold halter dress—simple yet elegant and modest—hoping to make a good first impression on his family. She'd opted not to attend the rehearsal dinner with Cody last night since Frank had advised her to keep a low profile while here in Reno. They didn't want word to leak that she'd left Stateline. Cody's dad felt the wedding was private enough, but she couldn't deny her nervous feelings about meeting the rest of Cody's clan.

"The bride doesn't stand a chance of being the most gorgeous woman at the wedding." Cody drew her arm through his elbow and led her to the car.

"Guess where the rehearsal dinner was," he said as she settled into his Jeep.

"That restaurant where I met your dad?"

"Yep, Bertha Miranda's. I told you it's the family fav. No wedding would be complete without a little of Bertha's cooking. Both Frankie and Delanie had their rehearsal dinners there, and now Brady. And someday maybe. . ." Cody sent a meaningful glance in her direction. Her heart warmed to the idea.

She opted for a safer subject. "Remind me again who's who."

Cody backed out of the driveway. "There are four of us. Frankie, or Frank Jr., is the oldest. He is married to Sunni, and they have two kids—"

"Summer and Mason."

"Good memory." He stopped at the stop sign and looked both ways. "They are four and six. Brady, the second child, is marrying Kendall today. Her parents are missionaries in Mexico."

Lexi felt intimidated by that. Missionaries gave up everything for others. They were the antithesis of Lexi's family.

"I'm number three, and after tonight will be the only single sibling. The baby and only girl is Delanie. She and her husband, Eli, are both cops and the proud parents of Camden—a baby boy born earlier this year."

"Sounds like a nice family." *Nice and too perfect for the likes of me.*

Lexi had wished a million times for brothers and sisters. Instead, she had nannies and a lonely life except for her wonderful summers with Gram and Gramps.

❧

Once they arrived at the designated wedding spot, Cody made some quick introductions to those who were around— Frankie, Sunni, and Eli. He left Lexi in the shade of a tree talking with Sunni. As the best man, he had obligations to fulfill, but at the reception, other than the toast, he'd be a free man. Free to spend time with the woman he loved.

When he and Brady drove up on the golf cart after pictures had finished, he spotted her immediately. His gut curled at the sight of her. She was beautiful with her hair pulled up, leaving her long ivory neck exposed.

As he approached, their gazes locked. She smiled.

"Hey." He kissed her cheek. "Have you been okay?"

"Fine. You look good in that penguin suit."

He spun around so she could get the full effect. Lexi laughed. "May I seat you, mademoiselle?" He held his arm out, and she linked hers through. Frankie and Eli had already begun seating the early arrivers.

He led her down a grassy knoll. White chairs had been lined up facing a small lake. The weather was perfect, and the setting couldn't have been prettier, green grass in every direction with flowers and trees to accentuate the beauty. An occasional jogger ran past on a nearby path. He guided Lexi all the way to the second row on the groom's side. Sunni, Frankie's wife, was already seated there, and she scooted over one chair.

"I'll see you after." He placed another light kiss on her cheek.

Each time Cody ushered someone to a seat, his gaze was drawn to Lexi. She was, by far, the most beautiful woman at the wedding, and she was there with him!

Finally it was time for the ceremony to begin. Brady took his place next to the minister. The music changed. Frankie walked their grandmother down the aisle. Now it was Cody's turn to walk their mom down the aisle. Then Eli led Kendall's mom to her place in the front row.

Cody took his place at Brady's side. Frankie and Eli sat in the front row next to his parents.

Cody's eyes rested on Lexi. She smiled. In his heart grew tender shoots of love. She was it. He didn't know the whens or hows, but he knew—she was the one. Reflected in her expression was the same wonder he experienced.

❧

Lexi took in every detail of the wedding. There was no glitz but a sweet serenity. As she tried to imagine her parents at such an event, she knew the simplicity would appall them, but honestly, if her day ever came, this couldn't be more perfect. She'd been to a few big celebrity weddings but nothing like this. There were only sixty or so people—all close friends and family. No one on the A-list showed up, no who's who among great American people, but it was precious nonetheless.

After Summer and Mason, Delanie walked down the aisle. She wore a brown dress trimmed in pink. Sunni whispered to Lexi that, sadly, Kendall's lifelong friend was ready to deliver a baby any day now and was unable to make the ceremony. A flutist began to play a classical song. Mrs. Brooks, the bride's mother, stood. The crowd followed suit.

Kendall, on the arm of her father, started down the mound toward her guests gathered at the end of the walk. A lump gathered in Lexi's throat. She wasn't even sure why.

Kendall was beautiful in her white gown. Her dad looked proud. Lexi turned to watch Brady. Love poured out of his expression. A tear rolled down Lexi's cheek. She blinked, not wanting to create a train wreck with her makeup. Cody seemed more than willing to love her like that, but she wasn't worthy of such a nice guy. How disappointed his parents would be if they knew the truth about her.

When Kendall reached the end of the aisle, Brady stepped out to meet her. The minister asked who gave this woman, and her dad said, "Her mother and I do." He then raised the sheer veil, kissing her cheek.

Another tear escaped, and Lexi wiped it away.

Kendall's father placed her hand in Brady's and squeezed Brady's shoulder as he moved toward his seat beside his wife in the front row.

Lexi's lips quivered. Her family was so broken. Her dad would never willingly hand her over to a firefighter from

Tahoe. He really didn't care if Lexi married or not, but if she did, he hoped for a power marriage to a man in the entertainment industry.

Lexi shifted her attention back to the pastor and his message. "It's much easier to fall in love than to stay in love. Staying in love requires strategy, commitment, and endurance." He paused, his eyes scanning the audience. Lexi would have sworn they settled on her.

"The strategy is loving each other in daily living, in the small stuff as well as the big. Kendall and Brady, if you don't have a plan and work at it, you will end up in a rut and possibly even with a love that's grown cold. Loving well requires making each other's needs a high priority. It means figuring out how the other feels valued. Strategically keep your marriage above all else in this life—work, kids, friends, hobbies. Keep God on the throne and marriage right under Him. If you live out this strategy, your marriage will be a great source of comfort, joy, and peace.

"Commitment is more than resignation to stick this out until the end because marriage is until death. Commitment is the other side of the same coin, determining this is for life and then making the relationship the best it can be—for the Lord and His glory, for each other, and for the peace that type of commitment brings.

"Last but not least is endurance. This is not a sprint but a long haul. The Bible speaks of love enduring all things, and that is certainly a part of it. Endurance means dealing with sickness, hardship, a job loss, economic crisis—the list goes on. Endurance takes the race one step and one day at a time, always moving toward the long-term goal of survival and finishing the race set before you. But do more than finish—finish well. Finish with victory. Finish with joy. Finish with a flourish."

Lexi pondered the pastor's words while he went on with the wedding vows. *Where do I go from here? I had one goal, to model, and that has ended.* She felt purposeless, but a part of her was also relieved. Definitely a part of her was ready to move on, but to what?

She refocused as Brady recited his vows with a deep, confident voice. "When I found the one my heart loves, I held her and would not let her go. Kendall, I will hold you through good times and bad. I will not let you go whether we are rich or poor, sick or well. I will cherish you and honor you all the days of my life."

The tender words intensified the ache in Lexi's heart. She glanced at Cody, and his eyes were on her. She couldn't deny that she wanted him to be part of the long-range plan, a part of her tomorrow. But with this whole arson thing hanging over her head, did she even have a tomorrow? Fear knotted her stomach. This might turn out worse than anyone anticipated.

nine

As the wedding party exited, Cody winked at her. He affected her in gentle ways she'd never experienced. The parents followed the bridal party, and then Lexi's row exited.

Cody grabbed her by the elbow as soon as she stepped off the grassy area and onto the pavement of the parking lot. He grabbed Sunni with his other hand. "The wedding party still has a photo shoot. Since Lexi knows no one, would you mind if she hangs with you until we get done? Maybe she can ride with you to the clubhouse where the reception will be held."

"Of course."

Lexi and Sunni spent some time talking during the short drive. She was quite interested in Lexi's life of fame and fortune, wanting to hear all about whom she knew, where she'd been, and why in the world she was at a small-town event in Reno.

"I've been to a few Hollywood weddings, and not one compares to this."

Sunni rolled her eyes. "Please don't tell me they got to you, too."

"What are you talking about?" Lexi couldn't follow her train of thought.

"The holy Coopers." Sunni raised her brow and cocked her head, daring Lexi to deny it.

Lexi felt offended for the family. "They don't seem that way to me. Don't you think they are genuine?"

"I suppose they are genuine enough. I just don't think like

they do. Don't get me wrong, I'm a Christian, too. I just don't eat, breathe, and sleep God."

Sunni parked her Impala in front of the clubhouse. They were among the first to arrive. As they walked to the open-air ramada where the reception was set, Lexi continued. "I don't either, but I'm trying to learn. I've done it the other way, and believe me, I've made a bigger mess out of my life than you could ever imagine. I guess you could say one of my biggest regrets is leaving God in my childhood along with pigtails and missing teeth." An ache of remorse filled her heart.

"Why? You've had a great life." Sunni seemed dumbfounded by Lexi's statement. They studied the seating chart and found their assigned seats.

"I have had a great life—by the world's standard. I've had many privileges few are afforded. But you know what I missed? The joy, the peace, the contentment." Her vision blurred slightly. "It's an empty world. You have no idea how lucky you are. A husband who loves you. Two great kids. A family to lean on."

Just then Frankie arrived with Cody.

"Pictures over already?" Lexi asked.

"A few family poses left, so we are going to steal Sunni. Be right back." Cody kissed Lexi's cheek, and the sound of a camera clicked somewhere off in the distance.

The reception was fun. After a nice dinner, Cody introduced Lexi to every guest. They did a couple of line dances and the Funky Chicken. Lexi had a great time and even forgot the trouble hanging over her head.

Dusk was settling, and little tiki lamps were lit. Cody led her to the edge of the dance floor for their first slow dance. He pulled her close, and she draped an arm on his shoulder. Several flashes went off from somewhere beyond the ramada.

"Are you enjoying yourself?" Cody asked as he began a slow two-step.

"Very much. It's the best wedding I've ever attended."

He missed a step, and she almost got his toes. "Really?"

"You sound shocked."

"I am. I thought it might seem rather plain to you. I mean, after all, you've attended some pretty glitzy events."

Lexi laughed. "You sound like your sister-in-law. Most of those events were exciting, even glamorous, but I left feeling empty at the end of the night."

"I'm glad you don't feel that way tonight." With both hands on her back, he drew her against him. His feet stopped as his lips found hers.

Dazed, Lexi opened her eyes at the end of the tender moment. Another flash went off in the dusk beyond the dance floor.

"How many photographers did they hire anyway?"

Cody shrugged. "I think just one and an assistant."

"Seems every time I turn around there are lights flashing." Reality hit Lexi with brute force. "How could I be so stupid?"

"What are you talking about?" Cody's brows drew together.

"The paparazzi. They're here."

Cody glanced around. "I don't see anything."

She hugged him close and whispered near his ear. "Walk with me and act normal."

Taking his hand in hers, she led him off into the darkness just beyond the ramada. *How did they find me?* She didn't know who she was madder at—them for showing up or herself for letting her guard down. She was very camera conscious in LA, but she didn't think she'd need to be in Reno. Once she'd left modeling behind and told no one of her destination, she'd foolishly assumed she was no longer a walking target.

⁂

Cody's senses were alert, but he neither heard nor saw anything. She stopped near the edge of the darkness. "Kiss me more, Cody. I've waited all night." She held up a hand, indicating he shouldn't move.

Then she let out a little groan. Flashes lit up the darkness like fireworks on the Fourth. Cody ran toward the closest—only twenty feet or so away behind some bushes. He grabbed the scoundrel by the throat. "What do you think you're doing?"

"Earning a living, buddy."

Cody grabbed his camera.

"Hey, that's mine." The guy tried to grab it back.

Cody yanked and overpowered the guy. "Not anymore." He tossed the camera to Lexi. "Get the memory chip out."

"Won't do you any good. There were three of us out here. You're only getting a third of what we took."

Cody shook the guy. "You scoundrel. You have no right." He longed to punch him square in the face.

"I have as much right as you to earn a living."

Lexi shoved his camera at him. "Not exploiting people's lives, you don't."

Cody grabbed the camera. "Call your friends back over here. You want your equipment back? We need their memory chips, too. We'll erase them and mail them back to you."

"Look, man. They're not coming back."

Cody yanked the guy's cell phone off his belt. "Call them. This is my brother's wedding, and you have no right to take advantage of it."

"We don't care about your brother." He punched in a number. "We're here for her." He pointed at Lexi. "Yeah, dude, they want your memory chips. They're holding my camera hostage."

He paused. Laughed. "Cool. Thanks. I owe you. They'll be right here with the ransom."

Two other young punks showed up in a matter of minutes. Each handed Cody a memory chip. Suspicious, he decided to check them out and make sure they held the pictures of the wedding. He slipped each one into the camera that he still held in his possession. "Yep, sure enough—these are it."

"I'm hurt, man. You don't trust us," the guy with the spiked hair stated in a deadpan voice.

"Give me an address, and I'll ship these back to you."

"Don't bother, man. Keep them as a souvenir of the time you almost made the tabloids. Some would consider that an honor."

"An honor?" Lexi laughed. "Hardly."

"So what's up with you anyway?" The second guy who came back questioned Lexi. "You trading in the LA scene for this dude?"

"My life is none of your business." Lexi glared at him.

"I think it's time you guys hightail it out of here." Cody eyed each of them. "And don't come back. Not tonight, not ever."

They all looked at each other and shrugged. "Guess we're uninvited." Then he looked directly at Cody. "My camera?"

Cody handed it over.

They all walked out into the darkness.

"Cody, I'm so sorry. I had no idea. I feel terrible. No wonder your dad advised me to keep a low profile here in Reno."

He took her hand, and they walked back to the reception. "Hey, it's over. At least we weren't blindsided at the checkout counter with us on the cover. That's why my dad insisted you miss the rehearsal dinner. He hoped the wedding would be a more private affair with less chance of exposure, but thankfully, no one ever has to know. The near darkness and loud music left everyone unaware." He glanced over the unsuspecting crowd. "And I'm glad he agreed you could be my date tonight." He kissed her cheek.

"Me, too, but I'm sure you know that whole paparazzi thing has happened to me before—more than once. And not only do they twist the truth, but the worse they can make a person sound, the happier they are."

Cody guided Lexi back to their table. He held out the chair, and she tucked her dress neatly under her and settled in. "Well, you've gotten to know my family over the last few hours. What do you think?"

"They are all very nice."

"I think I hear a 'but' in there somewhere. Very nice, but. . ."

Lexi squirmed under his scrutiny. She seemed to consider her words with care. "I just can't help but wonder what they think of me. I mean, they are all warm and kind, but they must be questioning what a nice guy like you is doing with a girl like me."

"A girl like you. . ." He ran his gaze over her. "A girl who is beautiful. A girl who is sweet. A girl who makes me glad to be alive." He placed his index finger under her chin, lifting her head, and placed a quick kiss on her mouth. "Yeah. They must think I'm crazy. Not much about you to admire. Not much at all."

Lexi's face grew serious. "You know what I mean. I come with all kinds of baggage, very public baggage. And to top that, I come with men stalking me, and by association your family, with cameras."

"Lexi, they'll grow to love you, just as I have, and none of it will matter."

Love me? You love me? He was still talking, but she had no idea what he was saying. She hadn't gotten past the fact that he said he loved her. He loved her! Wow! No man had ever said he loved her before. Cody said it so casually, so matter-of-fact that maybe he didn't mean it the way she was taking it. She was making too big a deal out of words spoken without fanfare.

"Excuse me." One of the waitresses tapped Lexi on the shoulder. "A guy with spiked hair who said he was your personal photographer asked me to give you this." She held out an envelope.

Lexi's stomach dropped to her shoes. With dread she reached out and accepted the offering. "Thank you."

Cody watched her with curiosity as she tore open the plain white square, pulling out a folded paper from inside. With trepidation she unfolded the note and laid it in front of her. She squinted to read the scribble in such dim light. *Sucker, we'd already downloaded two of the three memory chips. See you around—literally. At every supermarket in the country.* Lexi closed her eyes and sighed.

Cody grabbed the note. "That creep. I'd like to beat the snot right out of him."

Boy, did Lexi understand that sentiment. "Still think your family will *love me*?"

"I won't lie to you—this will upset them, but it's not your fault. They won't hold it against you personally."

"Should we go tell them?" Lexi started to rise.

Cody placed his hand on hers. "Let's wait for tomorrow's luncheon."

"Luncheon?"

"Tomorrow my parents are hosting our immediate family along with Kendall's for a lasagna lunch and gift opening."

"Aren't they going on a honeymoon?"

"They are, but since her parents live in Mexico, she wanted them to be part of the gift opening celebration before they left to go back. Brady and Kendall will leave for Maui the following morning."

Lexi tried to get back into the mood of the festivities, but the articles and implications to come had now overshadowed the joy of the event.

The following morning, Lexi helped Mrs. Cooper get ready for the luncheon. She scrubbed vegetables, chopped a salad, and made some ranch dressing. She was grateful for the time she had spent with Gram in the kitchen. At least she had some skill.

Lexi fought the urge to blurt out the news. Her promise to Cody to let him tell his family was the only thing keeping the news at bay. Lexi wasn't good at waiting. She just wanted things over with.

Cody was staying at Brady's apartment since the place was empty, and he hadn't arrived yet. His mom was easy to be with and talk to, so she didn't mind. Besides, Chief Cooper wanted her to stay through the following weekend. That would be ten days total away from the fire mystery.

She and Cody had called her grandparents several times, but unfortunately and fortunately, no more fires had been set. She knew this only made her appear guiltier. She tried not to think about it to avoid the stress and tension.

"Mom, you're not going to believe this," Frankie said on his way in through the front door.

Lexi spotted a newspaper in one hand and a grocery bag in the other. Her stomach knotted. *Cody, where are you?*

"Pictures of Brady's wedding are in the newspaper this morning."

He sounded excited. Lexi hoped the rest of the family

would feel that way.

"What?"

"They are really focused more on Lexi than Brady and Kendall." Sunni set another bag on the island next to the one Frankie plopped down. She picked up the paper her husband had just laid down and flipped it open to the local news section. "Here it is."

Mrs. Cooper stopped in the middle of her lasagna prep, wiped her hands, and picked up the paper. Lexi watched as Cody's mom glanced over the article.

"What did it say?" She didn't want to ask but had to.

"Not much." Mrs. Cooper held the paper out to her. "But what it did say wasn't terribly nice."

Lexi accepted the paper. "It never is."

The title was "Saints and a Sinner." Lexi read the caption, guessing where this was headed.

It talked about the fact that yesterday Police Chief Frank Cooper's son married a missionary from Mexico. Then it went on to say that while one son was marrying a saint, the other could be dating a sinner. Lexi laid the paper aside. "I'm sorry."

Mrs. Cooper gave her hand a reassuring squeeze. "Lexi, we are all sinners. There isn't a saint among us, nor is there a reason to be sorry. This isn't your fault."

How did his mom always know just the right thing to say? "Thanks. I appreciate your kind words of encouragement."

His mom smiled. "They aren't just kind words—they are truth."

When Cody arrived, Lexi filled him in. He took his parents aside to let them know this one article in the Reno paper probably wouldn't be the end of it. They both looked concerned, but neither condemned. Each hugged Lexi, reassuring her that they knew she'd put her past behind her and was moving into a solid future with God.

❧

After a weekend packed with wedding activity, Cody prepared to go back down to the mountain Sunday evening. "Can we take a walk before I go?"

"I'd love to." She focused on Mason and Summer who both wanted to start a fourth game of Candy Land. "Guys, I'm going on a walk with your uncle Cody, so you'll have to play without me."

They both protested, but Lexi stood firm in her resolve.

Cody held the door open for her, and she led the way out. "It's pretty out here this evening."

"It is. How are you holding up? You haven't mentioned the whole arson thing since we got here. You doing okay?"

"I'm all right. There's too much activity around your parents' place to think about much."

He nodded his agreement. "How about in the deep of night when there are no distractions?"

"How did you know?"

He pulled her against his side, wrapping his arm around her shoulders. "Your eyes, for one thing. The bags are tattling on you."

She acted incensed. "Don't you know that you never mention a woman's bags?"

"Don't try to change the subject. I know it's hard, but don't worry. I'm confident we'll get to the bottom of this whole thing."

"Lately my mind has been more on the tabloids than the fires." She stopped to sniff a rosebush.

"Mine, too, but it's out of our hands. We just need to move forward and not let it affect us."

"I'll try."

They walked on the trail that led to the lake. He stopped at a bench and pulled her onto his lap. "I'm going to miss you this week." He kissed her cheek near her ear.

"I hate to admit it, but I think I'll miss you, as well."

"Why do you hate to admit it?"

"I try not to get too attached." She ran her index finger over his jaw.

"I'm safe. You can attach to me." He kissed her, and the passion ignited. He stood. "I've got to get going, but know you'll be in my thoughts and prayers this week."

"And you in mine."

When they returned, Cody bid his family good-bye and headed for home. He thought about Lexi the whole drive, a grin plastered to his face. As he pulled into his driveway, he spotted a strange van in front of Alph and Essie's house. There were two men waiting at their front door. The moment Alph swung it open, the flashes were blinking.

Cody jumped out of his car and ran across the street. "What do you think you're doing?" He grabbed the guy closest to him by the collar of his shirt.

ten

Cody jerked the man away from the door. "Get out of here right now! Both of you."

"Hey!" The middle-aged man still standing on the stoop faced Cody. "We're here for the story. Came to see if the grandparents or the boyfriend have a comment on the arson situation. Rumor has it they stopped once Alexandria left the area." The man was cocky, making Cody even angrier. "Comments?" He held out a mic.

"Leave now, or we'll call the police." Cody ground out each word.

"Your choice." The guy shrugged and strutted off. The other man—the one Cody had manhandled—had already climbed into the vehicle, but the cocky guy turned back before he entered the van. "I find a lot of irony that a pyromaniac is dating a fireman."

Essie clutched Cody's arm. "Don't give him the satisfaction. He isn't worth going to jail over."

Cody let out a long, slow breath, releasing some of his pent-up frustration. "You're right. I know you are. Are you two okay?"

"We're fine. Come in and tell us what in the world is going on. We saw some scenes from your brother's wedding on some entertainment show that gossips about the celebrities. They said some awful things about Lexi."

Cody hugged Essie. "I'm sorry, but you know their job is to create sensationalism, not tell the truth."

"Alph and I are worried that the fires stopped when Lexi left. Does that mean we are being watched day and night?"

"I don't know what it means, but you're right—it doesn't look good for Lexi. And now this." Cody let out another long sigh. "How am I going to break the latest news to her? You know it's only a matter of time before she'll hear the implications."

"She sounded worn out when I talked to her earlier today. How is she handling all this?"

Cody shook his head. "It's hard, and now it's going to get that much harder. I need to tell her, and I'd rather do it in person. You guys can pray for wisdom as we walk through this mess."

They both agreed, and the three of them prayed together before Cody headed home. In light of this latest episode, he now planned to head back into Reno tomorrow, which meant finding somebody to cover his shift. He decided to take the whole week off, even though he'd just returned from a three-day hiatus for the wedding. No telling what sort of difficulty they might run into this week as the gossip story broke. Since Lexi was a celebrity, there would be a lot more speculation than if she were a regular joe.

Cody spent the evening doing his laundry, on the phone with his dad, and in prayer. He wanted Lexi to have a really fun day and evening before he dropped this latest bomb.

The following morning, Lexi was home alone at his parents' when he arrived. He found her in the backyard reclining on a chaise lounge and reading a novel she'd borrowed from his mom.

❧

"Hey, beautiful." He held out a bouquet of tulips.

"Cody!" She laid down her book and accepted the flowers. "I thought you were working."

"I decided to take a week off and hang out with you." She studied him a moment, wondering if there was more to it. Then she decided just to take him at face value.

"I thought I'd give you a tour of Reno today. Not nearly as fun as a tour of Lake Tahoe, but it's something to do."

She really didn't care what they did, as long as they did it together. She wavered between feeling crazy about Cody and believing she was not worthy of him. Someday she'd have to settle on one or the other.

She went inside and slipped on a pair of tennis shoes, just in case they did a lot of walking.

"I'm going to give you some choices. Now, don't get too excited. We can go to Fleischmann Planetarium."

She scrunched up her nose. "Anything better than that?"

"Oh, it gets lots better. How about the National Bowling Stadium or the National Automobile Museum?" He raised his brows like he'd just offered her two fabulous choices.

"You're kidding, right?"

"I'm offering you the best of Reno, and you're turning me down?" He acted hurt. "Okay, my last offer is the Sierra Safari Zoo."

"It will do." She gathered up her purse and a sweatshirt and led the way to the door.

After they were in the Jeep and on the road, he said, "I was hoping you'd choose this place. I haven't been there since a school field trip, but it's really cool. It's up Virginia Street— farther north than Brady's apartment, and set at the base of Peavine Mountain."

"These things you people refer to as mountains are not much more than hills."

"Well, they aren't the Swiss Alps, but they're mountains, nonetheless."

"Ya think?" She liked to goad his hometown pride. "You ever been to a real mountain, like Big Bear in Southern California?"

"Heavenly is a real mountain." He gave her his stern look.

"You got me there."

They spent most of the afternoon traipsing through the zoo. Their lighthearted banter felt good after days of heaviness.

"I have to admit, this place far exceeded my expectations."

"May I say I told you so?" He opened the Jeep door for her.

"Seriously, I like the way they have the animals in their own habitats. And not your usual elephants and tigers."

"So, what now, my gallant chauffeur?"

"Well, I thought we might get a dinner and game night going with Delanie and Eli. Maybe Frankie and Sunni, too. What do you think?"

"Sure, why not?" His family would tolerate her for his sake.

❧

Cody dropped off Lexi at his parents' and ran to Brady's to change, shower, and set the evening's plans into motion. He felt torn, wondering if he should have told Lexi about the upcoming exposé on her activities since leaving LA.

How do you drop a bombshell on someone like that? *Honesty is the best policy.* His dad had said that a million times in their growing-up years. He knew he'd been less than honest with Lexi by not saying anything. He'd withheld information. As kids, that was viewed exactly the same as lying—a sin of omission instead of a sin of commission, but still a sin, his parents had assured them.

He and the Lord had a talk during his shower. "I'm sorry. I should have told her. I'll tell her as soon as dinner ends and everyone heads their separate ways. I don't want her to deal with that black cloud during dinner." The guilt pricked. "You're right. I need to tell her ASAP. I'll tell her on the drive over to the restaurant for dinner."

When Cody arrived back at his parents', Eli and Delanie were there. Eli said, "Thought we'd ride over with you."

"Where are we going?" Delanie asked.

"George's."

Delanie rolled her eyes. "You guys did that on purpose so you could watch the game tonight."

Cody shared a conspiratorial glance with Eli.

Lexi came down the hall, and as always, every glance at her made Cody feel like a lucky, lucky man. He smiled, and she returned it. There were no commitments or promises between them, but the fact that she'd softened toward him was enough hope to keep him going. They'd not verbalized much, but if he could read people at all, she was definitely interested.

Lexi greeted everyone, then the two couples exited the house and hopped in Cody's Jeep to go to the grill and oyster bar. Cody realized he wouldn't get the chance to tell her about the paparazzi until the end of the evening. Pulling her aside wouldn't be fair to her. She'd have no time to process or recover.

"Are Frankie and Sunni coming?" Delanie asked from the backseat.

"If they can get a sitter." Cody glanced in his rearview mirror at Delanie.

"Anybody hear from the newlyweds?" Delanie's eyes met his in the mirror.

Eli chuckled. "I'm thinking the family is the last thing on their minds."

When they arrived at George's, the girls headed for the restroom, leaving Eli and Cody to find a table. The place was loaded with televisions showing several different channels, depending on which direction you gazed.

When the girls returned, Lexi took the chair next to Cody, and Delanie settled on her right.

"What are you thinking?" Cody asked Lexi, not glancing up from the menu. He heard her gasp. His head jerked up, and following her gaze, he saw her face lighting up one of the large-screen TVs hanging from the wall. The sound was muted, but as they say, a picture is worth more anyhow.

The word *arsonist* with a question mark after it appeared across the bottom of the screen in bold print. There were photos of her grandparents and of Cody grabbing a guy by his collar and shoving him. Pictures of neighbors, their mouths moving. It didn't take much imagination to know what they were saying. Shots of the burned landscape after the fires that she supposedly set. A picture of his dad and his title printed out across the screen. Cody's name and title followed. Shots of the wedding.

Cody glanced at Lexi. Her hand covered her mouth, and abject horror filled her expression. The story lasted only a couple of minutes, but to Cody, it felt like at least two hours.

❧

Lexi couldn't believe this was happening. Her worst nightmare. Someone had leaked information to the tabloids about the fires. She'd been humiliated by the press before, but this had to be the worst of all time.

When they flashed a picture of Cody in front of her grandparents' home, shoving some guy around, her mortification grew into anger. He knew about this and didn't tell her?

"I need to go." Her tone was sharp and demanding.

Cody nodded. "I'm taking Lexi back to Mom and Dad's. We're going to bow out of dinner."

All four of them were caught up in the slide show of her life the past few weeks.

Delanie was the first to respond. "Of course." She hugged Lexi. "I'm so sorry." Her eyes held sympathy, and her words rang genuine. "If Frankie and Sunni don't make it, we'll just grab a cab."

"I hope this doesn't hurt your family in any way." Lexi's tone held regret.

Everyone said good-bye. Lexi kept her head low as they left the restaurant, praying no one would notice her. Cody held open her door and lingered after she'd climbed in.

"I'm sorry."

"For what?" Lexi snapped. "The exposé or the fact that you knew and didn't tell me?"

"It just happened last night." Cody kept his voice quiet.

"What were you thinking? That you, the big, bad Cody Cooper, scared them off?"

"I just wanted you to have a nice day—I planned to tell you tonight. Look, I know I was wrong, and I'm sorry. I should have told you first thing this morning—"

"This is why you came back down, isn't it?"

He nodded his head.

"Another lie! This is my life, my future. You don't have the right."

"I was wrong, and I admit it, Lexi. I asked you to forgive me."

She looked at him for a long time. "Here's the thing— people have been choosing what they think is best for me for a long time now. I never gave you that right."

Cody nodded and shut the door. She'd spotted the hurt in his eyes that her words had inflicted, but at this moment, her own hurt outweighed his.

The truth was, just like all the men before him—starting with her dad—they all thought they knew best. And with every one of them, trust had, sooner or later, been breached.

She'd known all along he was too good to be true. He was too nice, his family too nice.

When he stopped at the curb in front of his parents' place, Lexi turned toward him. "I want to go home—tonight. To my grandparents'. If you can't take me, I'll rent a car or call a taxi."

"I'll take you, but do you think that's wise?" She could barely make out his silhouette under the streetlamp.

"Don't worry, I'm not sticking around long enough to be accused of any foul play. I'm returning to LA tomorrow."

"But—"

"I'll hire an attorney or do whatever I need to do. I'm not staying here now that the whole world knows where I am."

Cody cleared his throat. "What about us?"

"Cody, there is no us and never was. You're just a nice guy who was there when I needed somebody. We had a few good times, shared a couple of sweet kisses, but that doesn't constitute an 'us.'"

He cringed at her honesty. Boy had he misread her. He climbed out of the Jeep, his heart hurting. He opened her door and followed her up the sidewalk to his parents' front door. "Just so you know, there was an us for me. It was real." He unlocked the front door, pushing it open. He stood back and waited for her to enter.

"Lexi! Cody!" His mom's voice greeted them. She was curled against his dad on the couch. "I thought you guys went out for the evening."

"We did."

Lexi excused herself, and Cody filled them in on the evening's events. His dad flipped on the television and surfed through the channels, but nothing about Lexi appeared.

Lexi carried out her things a few minutes later. The large

tote bag was hanging from her right shoulder, her purse on her left shoulder, and the smaller bag in her left hand. She stopped just inside the great room.

"I want to thank you both for your hospitality. You've been more than kind, including me in the wedding and everything. And thank you, Chief Cooper, for trying to help me."

Both of his parents rose and moved toward her.

"Lexi, I don't recommend this course of action."

"I understand, sir, but I can't stay here any longer. I have to regain control of my life and stop this downward spiral."

"I fear you may get hurt by that decision or make your situation worse." His brows drew together in concern.

"With the utmost respect, sir, how can it get worse? Here or at my grandparents', I'm a sitting target."

Cody's mom stepped between them and gave Lexi an extra tight hug. "You be careful. We'll be praying for you."

Lexi's eyes grew glassy. "Thank you." She squeezed his mom's hand. "For everything. I'm sorry your family got tangled in my web."

"Not to worry, dear. We'll be fine. It's you I'm concerned about."

Cody took the bags from Lexi and carried them to the Jeep. She followed, his mom holding her hand. His dad brought up the rear.

After Cody stowed the bags, they all hugged—everyone but he and Lexi. "Be safe, son. Call me." His dad stood by the driver's door, and his mom by Lexi's door. She spoke to Lexi in low tones.

The entire drive home was quiet. Cody contemplated the past six weeks or so since Lexi arrived. Who knew so much would transpire, but it had. He'd found and lost love in less than two months.

On the drive home, Lexi vacillated between knowing she deserved this and wondering why God hadn't intervened. Since the prodigal had returned to her God, life had gone from bad to worse. She had no idea where to turn from here and felt too numb to pray.

Cody's mom was a dear. She'd been kind in spite of everything. The last thing she'd said to her was how sorry she was that things didn't work out between Lexi and Cody. The woman should be sorry Lexi ever entered his life.

When they drove into her grandparents' driveway, the light from the family room window still glowed bright. Lexi wondered if they'd seen anything about her splattered across their television screen.

Cody unlocked their front door with his personal key. "It's just us," he hollered the minute he opened the door. Both Alph and Essie met them on their way to the family room.

"I'll get your bags." Cody went back outside.

Lexi settled on the couch in their family room, telling her grandparents what had transpired and why she'd come home. She heard the front door open and shut again. Cody's footsteps retreated the other direction. He must be putting her things in her room.

"I'm planning on returning to LA tomorrow."

Gram got teary, just as Lexi had expected, but she was fighting the urge to cry, which Lexi appreciated.

"I have to. If I stick around here, I could end up being charged for a crime I didn't commit." Her gaze roamed over each of the two faces that she loved most in the entire world. "I'll be back—soon. I promise."

Both of their expressions were skeptical, and Lexi hated that she'd given them cause to doubt her. Cody entered the room right before her promise, and his face reflected their same misgivings.

Lexi wanted to be mad that they'd question her integrity, but in truth, she knew she'd brought it on herself. This time she'd prove them all wrong. She'd be back before Christmas.

"Cody, will you record that celeb news show? I think it replays several times a day, and I want to know what they're saying about me."

Cody crinkled his brow. "You sure?"

She nodded. She knew by his expression that he thought she should leave well enough alone. He probably subscribed to the theory that what you don't know can't hurt you, but she knew better. In her business, knowledge was power.

eleven

"Lexi, Jamison. I was hoping you'd answer, but guess not. No hard feelings, I hope. Anyway, been seeing your mug a lot lately and have had several calls requesting you for one job or another. I've had to tell them you're no longer under contract, so I was hoping you'd grown weary and bored and would consider some new negotiations. Anyway, love, call me."

Lexi erased the message and closed her cell phone. Restless, she paced around the bed. She'd packed everything except what she needed in the morning. Even though they'd advised her not to leave the state, she had to get out of here. She'd called and secured a spot on a puddle jumper tomorrow afternoon, taking her from here to Reno and then a direct flight to LAX from there. She hated those little planes, but the sooner she could leave, the better. Besides, she didn't want to ask Cody for one more favor.

She glanced out her window, and his lights were still on. On a whim, she trekked across the street to see if he'd caught the story on her. She'd rather her grandparents not have to endure the humiliation if they didn't have to.

She knocked once. Cody's door swung open. He grabbed her arm, yanking her inside and slamming the door behind her.

"What are you doing out roaming around at this hour? In your mind, this situation may be over because you're leaving tomorrow, but you are still a suspect. You still need to keep a low profile, going nowhere alone."

His anger caught her off guard. Of course, she guessed that it stemmed a lot more from her leaving than her midnight wanderings. She'd said some pretty unkind things, and she'd take care of that tonight, too.

"You're right, but I couldn't sleep, and since your light was on. . ."

"So what did you need?"

"A cup of sugar." Her attempt at lightness failed. He didn't even crack a smile. *Right now I need one of your bear hugs.* But she'd burned that bridge. She wrapped her arms around her midsection.

"I wondered if we could check out your recording to see if you caught me."

Compassion filled his stern expression. "It's not worth watching. Take my word for it."

"Nonetheless, I need to." She chewed on her bottom lip. "Please."

He led her to his sitting area. The plasma TV hung above the fireplace, so she snuggled into his oversized sofa that sat facing the television. He picked up the remote, went to his saved list, and hit PLAY. He fast-forwarded to her part.

Lexi watched as pictures of her flitted across the screen. The reporter spouted off a lot of false information, including the fact that she'd been fired as a model. She just didn't want to do the kind of things Jamison had planned for her.

But the part that made her heartsick was the way they shed a negative light on the Coopers—how Reno's elected official had invited a suspected criminal into his home. They also shared the irony of Cody the firefighter taking a suspected arsonist into his arms and probably his bed. Scenes flashed of various kisses they'd shared.

"I'm sorry." She closed her eyes against the onslaught.

"Oh, they aren't through."

Pictures of the wedding flashed before her eyes and a tender scene between them. They went with the sinner-saint angle, asking if Cody would be the person to taint the family by marrying the wild woman and party girl Alexandria Eastridge.

Cody hit the OFF button, leaving a blank screen behind.

"You'd have been better off avoiding me like a bad disease." For the first time that night, Cody made eye contact.

"I won't argue that, just not for the reason you're implying."

He'd opened the door, but did she have the courage to be honest with him? She licked her dry lips.

"I didn't mean to hurt you, Cody." She pursed her lips, fighting the urge to cry. "For a brief moment in time, you and I were pretty wonderful together, but as you now know, I'd drag your whole family through the gutter." A couple of stray tears wound their way down her cheeks. "God may remove our sins as far as the east is from the west, but people remember far longer. And they are far meaner. In truth, my life has gotten far more difficult as I've attempted to return to God. Maybe it's futile. Maybe I'm too far gone."

"No one is too far gone. I promise you that. God redeems broken people and the years the locusts have eaten. He'll do that for you. Please let Him."

Cody went and retrieved a box of tissues for Lexi. She pulled one out and dried her wet cheeks. "I keep begging God to get me out of this mess, but things go from bad to worse."

"Don't beg, Lexi. Claim what you know to be true, and trust Him with what you don't understand. I know that sounds trite, but you are His beloved child. Believe it. Live like it. Nothing is allowed to touch your life unless God permits it. If He allows it, it's for your growth and His glory. Don't let the enemy win, but stand firm, knowing God will use this fire somehow in your life."

Several times during the last few minutes, Cody had started to reach for her hand but had stopped himself.

"I'm so sorry for everything. Please believe me." Fresh tears fell.

Cody drew his lips together in a tight line. She watched his Adam's apple rise and fall when he swallowed.

"I believe you, but this old heart of mine will need some time to heal."

She nodded. *Mine, too. Mine, too.*

She rose from the couch. "I'd better go. I have a 10:00 a.m. flight, so this is technically good-bye."

He stood and followed her to the front door. She stopped before opening it and faced him, wanting to pretend this good-bye meant nothing, but her tears betrayed her.

He opened his arms, and she stepped into them. He pulled her against him as she cried. She wasn't sure, but she thought she felt a tear or two drop into her hair.

❧

Holding Lexi hurt. Cody knew he'd see her again someday but wished he wouldn't. The pain was more than he wanted to bear.

He held her tight, careful not to speak any of the feelings he had for her. When he could bear it no more, he loosened his hold. "I'll walk you home. Promise me you'll stay put, no matter how restless you feel."

She nodded. "I promise." When she looked up at him, her face mere inches from his, he backed out of the embrace and took a deep breath.

"Let's get you home."

He set the pace at a brisk walk, not desiring a slow saunter with chitchat. Before going inside, she kissed his cheek. "Good-bye, Cody." Her tone rang with finality.

"Good-bye, Lexi." *I'll miss you more than you know.*

She seemed to want to say more but didn't. She opened her French door and waved at him before closing it. He stood there a minute. "Good-bye, Lexi," he whispered, turning to cross the street. He glanced back once. "God's best to you."

Cody hit the sack, too tired even to think. Time healed all wounds. He guessed he'd discover if that quotation carried any truth. Right now it felt like the biggest lie on the planet.

Cody's phone rang, startling him awake. He groped for the light and found his phone. It was the fire station.

"Another fire."

Cody jumped out of bed, grabbing a pair of jeans.

"Just a few houses from yours. Same chick."

"Thanks." He shut his cell and slipped on his Nikes. The clock said two thirty. He hadn't been asleep long. He ran out the door and across the street. He could see the fire trucks and headed over there.

"I saw the Newcombs' granddaughter walking down the road at about two."

Cody's heart dropped. A tiny doubt crept in, and he hated himself for it.

A young cop took Mrs. Stark's account and a description of what the suspect was wearing. The exact same outfit Lexi wore to his house. A navy velour jogging suit. He felt sick and leaned against the fire truck, trying to process everything.

Not one fire the whole time Lexi was in Reno, and her first night back, one was set with an eyewitness account. "God, what does this mean?" There were many facets to Lexi; he sure hoped pyromaniac wasn't one. His uncertainty increased as he listened to the report.

"About fifteen minutes after she walked by, I got worried. I mean, I'd heard the stories. I woke up the mister and dragged him outside with me, just in case she was still out there. That's when we saw the flames and called you."

"Good thing you did. Otherwise someone's home could have gone up in a blaze."

"Oh, I know. We've all been a little on edge, and with good reason, so it seems." She shook her head in disgust.

The fire was extinguished quickly, and after questioning the witness, the cop requested a search warrant. By the time Cody had walked toward his cabin, two police cars were parked in front of Alph and Essie's, their lights flashing.

Cody intercepted them. "Let me call and wake them. They are elderly, and Alph's heart isn't in great shape."

"Go ahead, but they need to come straight to the door." There was an officer on each side of the cabin. Cody didn't ask but was certain they'd even stationed one at the back door.

"Alph, it's me. I'm out front with a few of Douglas County's deputies. Can you come to the front door?"

The windows began to light up as Alph traversed the path from his bedroom to the front door. He answered in his robe, thin white legs sticking out below the hem.

"Sir, we have a search warrant." He held out a faxed document.

Alph nodded, opening the door wide. His eyes sought out Cody. He looked pale. Cody led him to his chair. "Wait here."

By the time he'd caught up with them, they were entering Lexi's room, shining the flashlight in her face.

❧

A bright light penetrated Lexi's sleep. She tried to open her eyes, but they quickly closed against the offensive brightness.

Her mind wouldn't wake up. She squinted and opened one eye slowly. Blinking, she tried to understand. A flashlight? She screamed and sat up, holding the covers tight against her chin.

A man behind the bright light read her the Miranda rights. *Dear God, no. Please let this be a bad dream.* Her heart raced, and fear gripped her.

Another cop flipped on the overhead light. She blinked, trying to get her eyes to adjust. He rifled through her room, stopping short at the overstuffed reading chair in the corner of the room.

"Can you read the description of what the suspect was wearing?" He stood, staring at the clothes Lexi had removed just a couple of hours ago.

As the policeman with the flashlight read the outfit described by the eyewitness, Lexi's gaze darted to the perfect match draped over the upholstered chair.

The guy by the chair motioned his partner over. "Think we've got a match."

Both officers studied the jogging suit without touching it. "Yep. Book her."

He whipped out a pair of handcuffs and yanked her from the bed. Before Lexi could protest, her hands were secured behind her back. Lexi was thankful the nights were cool so that she was wearing her long-sleeved flannel pajamas.

Cody stepped into the room. "Is that necessary? She's obviously not a flight risk."

He was dismissed with a glare.

Cody's gaze met hers. She saw sadness, confusion, even doubt. "I didn't do anything. Cody, you have to believe me. I never left here after you walked me home." If he didn't trust her, who would?

He nodded. "I'll call my dad."

The police led her outside and shoved her into the back of the squad car. The sight of her grandparents on the porch broke her heart. Would she never stop hurting them? Tears came again. *God, where are You?*

&

"Dad, it's me."

"Another fire?" he asked, sounding groggy.

"Yep. Lexi swears she didn't do it. I walked her home about 1:00 a.m., and an eyewitness claims to have seen her around two. She described her down to the outfit she'd had on earlier that night. When the cops entered with a search warrant, the exact outfit lay draped over her chair. An eyewitness is hard to dispute."

"Yes, it is, son. Yes, it is."

Cody could hear his mom in the background, probably wondering who was calling at three in the morning.

"I'll be there in a couple of hours."

"Thanks. I'm staying with her grandparents just to be certain they're all right. Come there, and we'll ride over together to the sheriff's office."

"Will do. And, son, we'll get to the bottom of this."

That's what he was afraid of—that when all was said and done, Lexi would be found guilty. *Love believes all things, hopes. . .* He felt like a fair-weather friend. Once things got complicated, he stopped believing in her. He tried to fight his rising doubt, but it assaulted him at every turn.

He returned to the house, finding Essie in the kitchen making hot chocolate. He knew being busy was her way of coping. Alph was in his chair staring straight ahead. His health concerned Cody.

He settled in the corner of the sofa, near Alph's chair, reaching out and patting the wrinkled arm. "My dad's on his way. He'll do everything he can to help Lexi."

Alph nodded. Essie carried in three mugs and passed them out. The silence screamed of Lexi's guilt. The ticking of the clock nearly drove Cody insane. The worst part of this whole nightmare was the toll it would take on her grandparents.

After what seemed like forever, the doorbell rang. Cody startled then jumped up to answer it. Both of his parents stood on the stoop. The night sky showed the first light of day.

He stepped aside to let them enter, and his mom hugged him tightly. His dad joined in, wrapping his strong arms around both Cody and his mom.

"I'll let her grandparents know we're heading over to the jail."

"I'd like to say hello." His mom followed him back to the family room.

She hugged each of them, placing a kiss on each of their cheeks.

"It doesn't look good for our Lexi girl, does it?" Alph's voice was hoarse. Cody knew he wrestled with a lump in the center of his throat. He'd fought one of those himself several times the past couple of days.

"Don't you worry—Frank will solve this mystery. We all know Lexi is innocent."

How I wish I knew that.

"Can I make a pot of coffee for you or some breakfast?" Essie offered.

"Maybe later. I want to get over to the sheriff's station and encourage Lexi, but we'll come by again before we head back to Reno."

They said their good-byes. On the way to his dad's truck, Cody said, "Mom, you are something else. I wish I had your faith in people, your exuberance, your compassionate heart."

He climbed into the backseat of the double cab.

"I see all those things in you, much more than I see them in myself. Look at you, willing to love Lexi in spite of her past. If that is not faith in people and a compassionate heart, I don't know what is."

His dad pulled back onto the main highway.

"The truth is, I don't want to believe she's guilty, but all evidence says otherwise. I'm doubting her, and I hate that I am."

"And add to the mix that you are in love with her." His mom read his heart so simply, so matter-of-factly. "That only increases the guilt and confusion."

"Don't be too quick to hang her. She's an intelligent woman. If she left your house to go start a fire, would she wear the same clothes?" His dad parked in front of the sheriff's office. "I don't think she'd make so many careless mistakes."

"Unless she wanted to get caught." Cody climbed out of the truck cab.

"Stop analyzing and start praying," his mom reminded. "Are you coming with me to see Lexi or with your dad to meet with the sheriff?"

"I'll go with you." Cody decided he needed his mom's encouragement as much or more than Lexi did.

She played her social worker card to get them inside the jail. A few minutes later, they brought Lexi in. She wore a bright orange outfit that resembled hospital scrubs. Relief settled on her face when she saw them.

"It's good to see familiar faces. Thanks for coming." She stopped just inside the small room, wishing for the freedom to run to them both and hug them tightly to her.

"Did you think for a minute we wouldn't?" Mrs. Cooper pulled her into a warm embrace. "Frank's here, too, and knowing my man, he has a plan. He'll have you out of here sooner than later." She kissed Lexi's cheek and then sat down at the table, opening her Bible.

Lexi and Cody followed her lead. Lexi took the chair next to her, and Cody sat across from them. Lexi glanced at Cody. Though she didn't deserve it, she needed to know he believed in her innocence. She searched his face.

He smiled at her, but it was a sad and pathetic one. Her heart dropped, as did her gaze. *He thinks I set those fires.* A lump lodged against her windpipe as a little piece of hope died.

twelve

"God reminded me tonight on the drive up here about Paul and Silas and their imprisonment. Do you remember that story from the Bible?" asked Mrs. Cooper.

Lexi shook her head. Much had been forgotten during the last dozen years—too much.

"Just like you, they'd been imprisoned, but on top of that, they'd been beaten as well. They didn't complain or even question God. They prayed, they worshipped, and they sang praises to Him. While they sang, an earthquake shook the prison, and the locked doors flew open."

Lexi wasn't sure where Mrs. Cooper's line of thinking was going. Did she think if the three of them sang loud enough the doors would pop open and she'd walk out a free woman?

"The truth is, we all have certain prisons in our lives. Not real jail cells, but there are times we all need deliverance from something. And if the act of praising God set Paul and Silas free, it will do the same for you and me." She began to sing a praise song.

The three of them spent the next thirty minutes or so worshipping the Lord. With each new song, Lexi felt stronger, less afraid. Her faith grew surer. She had no idea what would transpire in her life, but come what may, God would be with her. She knew that for sure at this moment.

"I am going to check on Frank and see if he's made any headway."

"Thank you." Lexi hugged Mrs. Cooper. The guard let her

out. Cody made no move to go, so Lexi returned to her seat at the table.

"Lexi, no matter how this thing plays out, I'm in love with you."

Her gaze jumped to him. Though she'd felt pretty sure he loved her, she hadn't expected him to make the big announcement to a girl in orange prison garb. His tender expression made her breath catch in her throat. He rose, moving around the table. His eyes never left hers. Her heart drummed against her rib cage. He reached for her hands, pulling her onto her feet. He placed a hand on each cheek, staring deeply into her eyes. "I love you, Lexi. Not only do I love you, but I want to marry you someday—if you'd say yes."

Lexi closed her eyes. *I love you as well, but we both know I'm not what you need.* A single tear squeezed through her tightly shut lids. He kissed it away. She fought the urge to turn her lips toward his. She stood still, not responding verbally to his proclamations. *Love is putting another's need before my own.* She'd read that somewhere. Today she'd love Cody enough to spare him the humiliation that would surely come if she stayed in his life for too long.

I love you, Cody, but you're way too nice for the likes of me. I've made lots of wrong turns. And you've avoided them. At least until you met me.

Lexi grappled with the irony. She'd had a lot of men she'd never wanted and had to walk away from the one man she truly did.

He held her close a few minutes. She didn't fight it, nor did she join in. Truth be told, she gained strength from him.

"I'll be back," he promised.

Lexi only nodded, but when he retreated, she wished for him already.

❧

Cody ached for her. He'd let the words of the praise songs seep deep into his soul. Like a man hungry for food, his spirit was hungry for the peace of God. The songs covered him like a soothing balm, washing away the trepidation of what was to come. Lexi was in God's hands, and that was where he'd have to leave her.

He searched for his dad and mom.

"I got her out." His dad was filling out paperwork. "According to NRS 193.155, if Lexi was truly guilty, the fires were only gross misdemeanors because the damage was less than $5,000."

"NRS?" his mom asked.

"The Nevada Revised Statutes. They could try to prove intent and charge her with more, but at this point, they won't."

"Only because of you?" Cody stated the obvious.

"Let's just say that in this world, who you know can help." He handed the paperwork to the woman at the desk.

"It'll be a few minutes. Have a seat." She pointed to the hard chairs lining the wall across from her area. The three of them did as they were told.

"So what now, Dad? What keeps all this from happening again?"

"I've been thinking, and I'm trying to come up with a foolproof plan. The thing is, somebody has to be watching her day and night. Probably the same somebody who notified the press where to find her in Reno."

Cody leaned across his mom so he could speak quietly, wanting no one to hear the uncertainties. "How can you be so sure it's not her?"

"I've been doing this job a long time. It's part gut instinct, part discernment from the Lord, and part looking past the obvious because it rarely is."

"So where do we go from here?" His mom turned her blue green eyes toward his dad.

"Somehow I've got to get her under twenty-four-hour surveillance. And that's where you come in." His dad's well-modulated voice was barely above a whisper. The three of them huddled closer. "I can use your house as a base for my operations. Eli just finished a big case he'd been on for months. They made a huge bust. Delanie is still on maternity leave. I'll see if they want to come visit you for a few days."

A jail guard led Lexi through the security door. She now wore the pastel plaid pajamas she'd had on when they brought her in. She had bedhead and no makeup but was a beautiful sight as far as Cody was concerned.

He went to her, pulling her into his arms and kissing her temple. Her hug was brief, and she pulled away, moving toward his parents.

"Thank you so much."

They both hugged her. His mom took her arm, and they walked to the truck together. She opened the back door and climbed in after Lexi. That left him to sit in the front with his dad. The morning sun was up, and Cody slipped on his sunglasses.

❧

"I need to figure out who is tailing you and why," Chief Cooper said.

Lexi glanced out the back window but wasn't sure which car he referred to. "You think I'm being followed?"

"Lexi, somebody is a step ahead of you. They have to be watching you at all times. I need you to think. Who would go to all this trouble and expense and why?"

Lexi shook her head.

They pulled up in front of her grandparents' house and unloaded. The front door swung open, and both Gram and Gramps met them on the porch. Their faces flooded with relief. They hugged her tight.

"Thank the good Lord," Gram said, taking her hand and leading her inside.

She glanced back, and Gramps motioned for the others to follow. They congregated in the family room.

Gramps turned to Chief Cooper. "Thanks so much for bringing our Lexi girl home." He shook his hand.

"Can I make everyone a nice breakfast?" Gram offered. "Mr. and Mrs. Cooper?"

"Only if you let me help. And it's Marilyn. Frank and Marilyn." She looked directly at Lexi. "Got it?"

She nodded and smiled. Someday some lucky woman would not only get Cody as a husband but would get Marilyn as a mother-in-law. Lexi had already grown to love her.

The two women headed into the kitchen. Gramps settled into his recliner. Cody and Frank both sat on the couch.

"Guess I'll help with breakfast." Lexi turned to leave, but Frank called her back.

"Lexi, I'd like to strategize with you. Do you mind staying?"

She shook her head and sat in Gram's recliner.

Frank turned to Gramps. "Do you have a garage?"

He nodded.

"And Cody also has a garage. That will help us smuggle people in and out."

"Who are we smuggling?" Lexi asked.

"I'm not sure yet. Depends on who's available. I'm hoping to keep it in the family and not involve the Reno PD. I think between Eli, Delanie, Frankie, and myself, we can get the job done. That is, if they are free and can help."

Gram and Marilyn carried in two trays, one with a pot of coffee and mugs and the other with cream and sugar. They set them both on the coffee table in front of the couch. Frank wasted no time pouring a cup and handing it to her. He continued filling mugs, and the women returned to their breakfast endeavor.

Lexi added a little cream to hers, feeling overwhelmed by this family and their kindness.

"What about the sheriff's office up here?" Gramps sipped the coffee Gram had doctored for him.

"They don't have the manpower, nor frankly, do they have a reason. They aren't, and I quote, 'wasting the taxpayers' money on a misdemeanor with an eyewitness.'"

"Then why are you?" Lexi had to know.

Frank shrugged. "You're a friend of Cody's, so you matter to us. Friends help friends. And it's personal."

"What do you mean?" Lexi set down her cup, giving Frank her full attention.

"I'm tired of people trying to ruin another person's life just because they can. I see it all the time in Reno. Vindictive hate crimes. They are a personal pet peeve, and I don't take them lightly."

Lexi smiled, relieved his answer had nothing to do with her future in Cody's life. "For my sake, I'm glad. I can't thank you enough."

"None of us can," Gramps added.

"It's my pleasure." Frank jotted a few notes down on a small pad he pulled from his front pocket.

"Cody, can we talk for a minute?" Lexi had to clear the air. His proclamation earlier today had been bugging her.

Frank looked up. "Do me a favor. Go stand out front.

I want the whole world to see Lexi is out, and it'll give me a chance to watch from the window and see who might be lurking in the shadows."

Lexi led the way through the front door. She walked over to Frank's truck and leaned on the bumper.

Cody asked her to move and lowered the tailgate. They both hopped on it, feet swinging above the ground.

"What's up?" His warm brown eyes probed her face.

"You are the sweetest guy I have ever met in my entire life."

❧

But. . . He heard it coming—the "let's be friends" speech. His heart hurt, but he'd try to be upbeat about the whole thing.

"You just have to know that I'm not feeling what you are."

He nodded.

"I don't want this whole grand gesture from your family because they assume that one day you and I will marry."

"I've never implied to anyone except you that we might marry." He hadn't intended for the defensive edge to slip into his tone.

"I'm glad. I think it's better that way. But I'd love it if we could be friends."

"We already are," he reminded her.

"Just so you don't expect more from me than I can give. You are the first guy in my life who seemed to like me for me. I got swept up in the idea that a man could care about me in a nonsexual way."

Cody nodded, praying this conversation would end soon.

"I'm sorry."

He forced a smile. "Me, too."

"You two coming in for breakfast?" His mom called from the open front door.

"Be right in," he called back. Relief poured over him. Now

he wouldn't have to listen to the same words—*You're a nice guy, but*—said fifty different ways. Cody slid off the tailgate.

"I don't want your family to dislike me, and if your dad no longer wants to help—"

"It's fine, Lexi." He wanted to say, "Maybe I was just caught up in the whole beautiful girlfriend idea." But he knew his motives were wrong, so he bit his tongue. Besides, it was a lie.

They joined the others at the table. Everyone's mood but his was celebratory. He needed some time alone to lick his wounds and regroup. But as his dad filled them in on his plan, Cody realized he'd have no time alone during the next few days. Not only that, but he'd be Lexi's watchdog by day— never leaving her side. This ought to be a thrill a minute.

"I'm not worried about her safety, so much. Whoever this is, the goal doesn't seem to be to harm, but some sort of revenge." His dad gazed at Lexi. "Has anyone ever threatened you?"

She shook her head.

"Blackmail?"

Shrugging, she laid down her fork.

"Ever been harassed by an ex-boyfriend, a jealous female friend, an old roommate?"

"Nope." Lexi pushed her barely eaten breakfast aside. Cody understood. The thought of food didn't settle well with him, either.

"Anyone angry with you, trying to manipulate you? Anybody want you back in LA?"

❧

Jamison. The thought hit Lexi like an avalanche.

"Who, Lexi? Who?" Frank was like a hound on a scent. "Somebody came to mind. Who was it?"

"Jamison Price, my agent."

"Why? What made you think of him?"

Every eye at the table was on her. They'd all stopped eating, waiting. "He wanted me to re-sign my contract with—" She paused, glancing at Gramps and then Gram. She searched for words that carried less meaning. "A different kind of modeling in mind." Cody's eyes were compassionate, encouraging.

Her gaze rested on Frank. "I wasn't interested, and he acted like he could care less, but I saw the pulsing jaw and knew he was angry."

"Has he contacted you since?" Frank's gaze was intense. Cody looked a lot like him.

"He left a message on my cell phone last night."

"May I listen to it?"

Lexi shook her head. "I erased it."

"What did he say? What did he want?" Frank's voice took on a demanding quality.

Lexi closed her eyes, trying to remember. "He said something about seeing my face a lot lately and that he'd had several requests for me. He thought I ought to come back to LA for some contract negotiations. I don't know exactly, but that was the gist of it all."

Frank asked for any info Lexi had on Jamison—address, phone numbers, full name.

"The more I think about it, the crazier it would be for him to be involved. He's a very rich man with a lot of clients. He doesn't have time for this sort of thing."

"Did you tell him you were coming here?"

She shook her head. "When I left his office that day, I had no idea where I was going."

Frank rested his elbows on the table. Everyone watched.

"He's processing," Marilyn whispered. She rose and started clearing plates. Gram joined her.

"Take a walk with me." Frank's gaze rested on Lexi.

"I'm still not dressed. Can you give me a minute?" Though her pajamas were beyond modest, Lexi didn't want to parade down the street in them. She'd already sat out front. That was bad enough.

After a quick change and shoving her mass of hair into a ponytail, she found Frank waiting at the front door. She dreaded what this walk might entail.

They walked for a few minutes in silence. Lexi knew Frank had his eye out for somebody tailing her. He reminded her of a cat about to pounce. All his senses seemed alert. She felt tightly coiled herself.

"Lexi, I need to ask some hard questions."

She shoved her hands into the long pocket on the front of her sweatshirt. "I figured you might, but I'll save you the trouble. Yes, in the past we had been—shall we say—more than friends."

"How long has he been your agent?"

"Twelve years."

"And when did things get personal?"

Lexi turned her head away, not wanting to see his reaction. "Almost immediately."

"How old were you?" She thought she heard disapproval in his tone.

She stared at the ground, watching it move with each step forward. "Sixteen."

"How old was he?"

"Almost thirty."

"That snake." Frank wrapped his arm around her shoulders and pulled her against his side. "Lexi, for all men everywhere, I am so sorry. Men like him should be castrated."

He did disapprove, but not of her.

"Who ended it and when?"

"I did. About five years ago."

"Good for you. How'd he take it?"

They'd circled the block and were heading back toward her grandparents' house. "He was angry—very angry—especially because I'd just signed another contract and still had almost five years left."

"After you refused to comply with his wishes, did your job assignments change? Did you get less work?"

"Yeah, but he blamed my age. I'd been doing a lot of teen-related shoots, a couple of music videos, that sort of thing, so I believed him."

The more questions he asked, the more certain he seemed that Jamison was behind the fires. She stopped next to her grandparents' mailbox. "Before we go back inside, I just want you to know how grateful I am that you're helping me. I could pay you."

He smiled. "I'm a public servant and not allowed to accept any sort of compensation, but even if I could, I don't want your money. I just want to help you get out of this mess." He paused to ask one final question. "Was your relationship with Jamison exclusive?"

thirteen

"Yes. There were no other men—until after." She focused on her shoe.

"How about for him? Were there others?"

She used her toe to move some gravel back and forth. "At the time, I didn't think so, but I found out later that he had slept with almost all his girls on a fairly consistent basis."

"I'd like to slap him with a few charges that have nothing to do with fires."

She raised her chin. "Me, too. He's hurt a lot of people."

"Did you ever think of turning him in?"

"Honestly, no. I grew up in the entertainment industry. This is not that uncommon."

Frank shook his head.

"I also wanted to assure you, you don't have to worry about me and Cody."

He looked surprised. "Who's worried?"

"Well, in case you are, don't be. I let him know this morning that we can only be friends."

"Friends, huh?" He studied Lexi. "Seemed like more than that to me."

She smiled, deciding to play it down. "I think he had a little crush on me."

"And you?" He watched her with that penetrating gaze.

She looked away, watching a bird overhead. "Me?" Searching for something cute to say, she drew a blank. Emotions hit her that she hadn't planned on. Tears she hadn't expected filled her eyes. "Me? I'm going back to LA and away from here just as soon as humanly possible." She glanced at her watch. "I'm booked on the 10:00 a.m. flight today." She attempted laughter. "Guess I won't make that one."

"If you leave, whoever is doing this to you wins."

She wiped at her cheeks. "I don't even know if I care. I just want away from here."

"Boy, do I understand that! If I were in your shoes, I'm sure I'd feel the same. But running rarely solves life's issues. Besides, this place isn't bad, but a man from LA might be."

"You're right." She sighed.

"Will you work with me on this for a few days and see who we can ferret out?"

She nodded. "I guess, but running holds more appeal."

He laughed. "I'm sure it does." He glanced at the house. "Don't run from Cody, either. If what I've observed is real, it's worth fighting for."

Lexi's tears refused to linger any longer. "Why would you want me in your son's life?"

"Grace, Lexi. God's amazing grace. We all have stuff in our pasts—stuff we regret and would like to erase. But God's mercies are new each morning. You've repented, you're forgiven, and you are a new creation in Christ. One I believe my son loves." He hugged her close, and they finished their walk to the front door.

Once they joined the others in the family room, Frank said, "Lexi, I'd like you and Cody to do something very public. Take a hike, whatever. I want as many people as possible to see you're out and about. In the meantime, I'll write a press release and have my office fax it to the Associated Press."

Lexi knew, though the walk fit into Frank's overall plan, he hoped it would accomplish more than just that. But she'd made up her mind. There was no going back.

"Since you'll probably be leaving in the next day or two and we talked about a ride up Heavenly on the gondola, how does that sound?"

A man who remembers his promises. "Sounds great. Give me ten minutes."

ea

Cody dreaded spending part of the day alone with Lexi. Not that he wouldn't love to be with her under different circumstances, but downshifting to just friends took more than a few hours. His dad used to say, *Fake it until you make it.* It was his way of saying—believe it, and your attitude will follow your actions. So, today he'd be the perfect friend. Not the man in love with her, not the man whose heart she just broke, but just a guy along for the ride.

He was foolish to actually think that Alexandria Eastridge—supermodel extraordinaire—would fall for him—Mr. Ordinary. Now thinking about it, he felt silly hoping she'd return his feelings. Nothing about them could ever work.

When Lexi finally returned, she smiled at him. He tried not to notice how good she looked and smelled. *Two good friends on an outing. Yep, that's all it was.* He opened the front door, waiting for her to exit first. *Doesn't have to be awkward. No sirree. Just two friends burning time.*

Cody drove them across the California line. Knowing she liked Starbucks, he stopped there first. *Good friends can be thoughtful.* "It will probably be cool up there, so I'm getting something hot." He ordered a large mocha latte.

She ordered a tall skinny mocha with no whip.

"Let's leave the car here and walk over. It's less than a block to the ticket booth." They passed by the quaint shops surrounding the resort. They very much belonged in a mountain town with their rugged wood exterior. Lexi stopped a couple of times to peer in windows.

"We've got time if you want to shop."

She smiled. Every time she looked at him, all he saw was sympathy in her eyes. He wanted to say, "Don't feel sorry for me. There are other fish in the pond." Of course he knew there weren't. For him, she was it. Her or nobody. *Looks like it'll be a long, lonely life.*

Cody bought two tickets for the gondola. Since it was a weekday morning, there was no line. The door on the side of the glass bubble opened, and they climbed aboard. He took one side, and she the other.

He wasn't going to say anything, but his chivalry reared its unwanted head. "The view is better from this direction."

"But you're going up backward."

"True, but I'm facing the lake."

"Ah." She moved over onto his bench, careful to leave space between them. "It's beautiful."

"No place prettier as far as I'm concerned."

≈

Lexi had always loved Lake Tahoe, but she couldn't express that to Cody when she said she couldn't wait to leave. The view was pristine. Blue in every direction—the sky, the mountains, the lake. "Thank you for bringing me here. I'd forgotten, and I'm glad I didn't miss this."

"We'll get off at the observation deck then ride on to the top. There is a little restaurant up there, and since you didn't eat much breakfast, I figure you must be hungry."

You're always taking care of me. "I am hungry, and I bet you are, too."

When their gondola stopped, Cody got out and offered his hand.

Habit, I'm sure. She accepted, and he steadied her as she climbed out. The metal beneath her feet wasn't solid, but a grate, providing a place for the melted snow to drain.

She clutched Cody's arm tighter. "Heights aren't my thing."

He wrapped an arm around her back. "My mom's, either, but it's worth the risk." He led her to view one landmark and then another as they slowly made their way around the entire deck.

"Every direction is beautiful in its own way."

"Yeah. This is one of my favorite spots on earth." He gazed out over the lake. "I come up here sometimes when I'm blue. I never leave that way. The beauty just lightens my load somehow."

That old familiar lump was back. He'd probably spend a few sad days up here because of her. How she regretted hurting him. If only she'd listened to her inner voice early on and kept a lot of distance between them. They'd both have been better off for it.

"Remember the praise lesson my mom shared with you this morning?"

"Was that only this morning? It seems like days ago." They were back to where they started on the circular deck that ran around a store and another building.

"I know." He gazed at the beauty surrounding them. "This very place was her first lesson in the power of praise."

"Really, how?" She wondered if his mom stood up here and praised God at the top of her lungs or something equally bold that Lexi would never have the courage to do.

"As I told you, she hates heights. She and my dad came up here for their anniversary the first year it was built. When she stepped off the gondola and onto this grate, her fear kicked into overdrive."

Cody led Lexi to a bench where they faced the lake. Lexi let go of his arm and held on to the gray vertical rails in front of her.

"Anyway, she and a group of women had been studying the power of praise. They called it warfare intercession or something like that. She decided to test it out—you know, kind of a rubber meets the road sort of thing?"

Lexi nodded.

"Just in her head, not out loud, she began to thank God that fear wasn't from Him. She began to claim what she knew the Word said about Him—like she could do all things in Christ. My dad said her legs stopped shaking, and she stepped out unafraid. She did spend most of her time up here mumbling under her breath to the Lord, though."

Lexi laughed. "Your mom is something else."

"That she is. My dad, too. He's a great guy with a heart of gold."

"Don't I know that. The whole family, really." *But most especially you.*

"You want to walk through the little store and then head on up to the top?"

"Sure." The store was tiny but chocked full of souvenirs, film, and candy. "Look, they take pictures." She'd really like to have their picture made with the lake in the background but didn't ask. It felt tacky after all she'd said much earlier this morning.

They got back into their bubble, as Cody called it, and floated up to the top. The restaurant Cody spoke of was an outdoor chuck wagon kind of place. The hostess led them to a table covered with an umbrella. The chairs were plastic and mismatched, but something about the place was quaint.

They each ordered a burger. There were Adirondack chairs

sitting around everywhere, filled with people.

Cody pointed to the chairs. "People ride up and spend the day. Some hike, some sit. There are usually several forms of entertainment—bands, magicians, whatever. One trail takes you even higher with a clear view of the entire lake."

The waitress brought their water. "Few more minutes on those burgers," she said before leaving.

"Do you want to hike after we eat?" Cody asked.

"I'd rather just claim a chair and watch the world go by. Do you mind?"

"No, we're both running on about two hours of sleep, so I echo your sentiments."

When the food arrived, they both concentrated on it rather than conversation.

After Cody paid the waitress and left a tip, he joined Lexi where she'd claimed two chairs facing the mountain. "So what now for you?"

She'd been asking herself the same question. "I'm not sure. Maybe some deep soul searching. Definitely a career change. I want nothing to do with modeling, acting, or music."

"Then I'm certain you are an atypical American. Isn't that just about everyone's secret dream—fame and fortune?"

"Why, Cody Cooper, I do believe that you are cynical, but it was my dream once, too."

"Was it? Or did your parents convince you it was?"

She thought about that. "I don't even know. It all started when I was so young. What came first, the chicken or the egg?" She shrugged.

"The nice thing is that I'm young enough to get a second chance. And I made enough money modeling to tide me over until I decide which direction to go. I read about a school in downtown LA where the kids have to pass through a metal detector to get in. Some students carry guns and knives. I want to find something that matters, make a difference in someone's life. Have an impact on the world for Christ. Just this morning, your dad reminded me of grace. I want to spread some grace around to others, the way God did with me." She paused and took a breath. "I'm sorry, I'm rambling and probably sound corny. Now you probably regret the question."

"No, no, and no to your previous observations."

Lexi grew quiet, enjoying the mountain air and the beauty. Her eyes grew heavy. She closed them—only for a moment. She was so tired.

❧

After Lexi fell asleep, Cody dozed off and on. She slept for about an hour, and he spent part of the time watching her—watching and wishing. When she opened her eyes, he said, "Welcome back, sleepyhead." He held out his hand. "Let's go home."

The ride back down was more comfortable, less awkward. Cody almost believed the friends thing might work. His aching heart, however, wasn't so easily convinced.

When they got back to her grandparents' house, her grandparents told them his dad had done a good job of getting the news out that Lexi had been released due to lack of evidence.

"I've already seen it on several news channels," Frank informed them. "This should turn up the heat. I also made sure to 'leak' the fact that she'd hired a personal bodyguard to stay with her at night. That way nobody will try anything until she's alone tomorrow morning. That bought me some time to get my plan into place and fully operational."

Lexi smiled at Cody. "Your dad has really gotten into this."

He nodded. "It's his job, and he loves it."

At dinner Frank filled them in on his plan. Between bites

of spaghetti, he told them that Eli, Delanie, and Frankie were coming down later tonight and bringing some borrowed police equipment with them. He was counting on whoever was watching Lexi to head home for a good night's sleep.

Everyone ate and listened intently.

"The sheriff agreed to thoroughly patrol the area at 4:00 a.m. He's checking every parked car along this block. If he doesn't find anything or anyone, then everyone will quickly man their posts and wait for daybreak."

Cody was impressed. His dad had drawn diagrams and printed maps of the neighborhood off the Internet. "Delanie will man the communications center, since she has Camden and can't be out in the field. I'll set it up tonight once they get here with the needed equipment."

It sounded like a fairly intricate plan to Cody. When they finished dinner, Lexi went in the kitchen to help her grandmother and his mom clean up. He followed his dad across the street to his A-frame cabin. "Dad, I've got two questions for you."

He stopped what he was doing. "Shoot."

"Do you really think Lexi will be safe? I'm worried about her."

"I'd never risk her safety. I promise you that, son. What is your second question?"

"Why are you so invested in this case?"

"Because I hate men who use women like this bum Jamison did. Once I prove he's behind this arson thing, I'm turning him over to LAPD for his sexual exploits with young women. I'm hoping he'll pay his dues behind bars."

❧

Frank and Marilyn spent the night at Cody's place. Frank asked Lexi if she'd mind trading spots with Cody so he could keep an eye on her. She and Marilyn shared Cody's king-sized bed. Frank slept just outside the bedroom door. "That way you have two eyewitnesses—just in case you need them. About five we'll send you home so you can prepare for your walk."

The next morning before the sun had fully risen over the mountains in the east, Lexi left her grandparents' home alone. Only she didn't feel alone because she had an earpiece with Delanie's voice in her head. She'd instructed her not to look to the left nor right, act normal, and set the pace as she typically would.

Her grandparents prayed for her before she left the house. She wore the same clothes she'd worn the other day. According to Frank, this should all go down like clockwork. She struggled to imagine Jamison going to all this trouble for her, but Frank seemed fairly certain.

She walked down the road and up and down several neighboring streets, winding her way back around toward home. Her path had been well planned, and Frank had placed people strategically along her way to watch out for her. She arrived back home with an uneventful walk behind her.

"Go on inside. My dad and Eli have a suspect in sight," reported Delanie. Lexi did as she was told, praying that this would finally be the end.

༄

Cody ran down the hill to the guy in the car his dad had spotted. By the time Cody got there, Eli had the guy spread-eagle across the hood of his older model Pontiac. His dad stood nearby.

"Who are you, pal, and who are you working for?" Eli demanded, handcuffing the guy. In truth, Cody knew by what his dad had said that they weren't in their jurisdiction but had received a special dispensation from the sheriff to arrest and book any suspects.

The guy was older and nervous. Cody figured he'd cave easily. "I was hired to tail some girl. Her boyfriend thinks she might be cheating on him, and fact is, she is with some firefighter dude."

"Who hired you?"

"That's confidential information. You should know that."

fourteen

His dad checked the man's cell phone. "Jamison Price was the last call you made." He glanced at Cody with a satisfied expression. "Who sets the fires?"

Eli raised the guy up off the car hood and turned him to face Frank.

"I said, who set the fires? Where's the girl?" his dad demanded in his best "bad cop" voice.

"I don't know nothin' about no fires, and the girl just returned home from her morning walk."

"Let me tell you something—you'd better tell us the entire job you're doing for Mr. Price, and you'd better tell us now. Otherwise, you could be brought up on charges a lot bigger than stalking." Eli tightened his hold on the guy's collar. "You hear what I'm saying?"

"Look, man, I'm a private investigator. I told yous before, I was hired to follow the model and report back to her boyfriend. Nuttin' more."

"When and how do you report?" Cody's dad asked.

"I call him every time she leaves the house. I let him know who she is with, what she is wearing, and where she goes."

"That's it?" Eli demanded.

The guy looked puzzled. "It's all he wanted. I'm full service—whatever my client wants, my client gets."

"Delanie, we need all eyes back out there. We have a Lexi look-alike on the loose somewhere toting a book of matches.

And notify the sheriff." Then Frank turned to Eli. "Leave him cuffed."

Eli informed the private investigator, "We'll be back for you soon. In the meantime, relax and enjoy a beautiful day."

"You guys got my phone. And I'm still cuffed. Hey, come back here!" he yelled.

"Dad, two streets over, the sheriff got a call reporting a Lexi spotting," said Delanie. "They want the sheriff to check it out."

"We're on it." The three of them sprinted, following Delanie's directions. Eli and Cody rounded the corner neck and neck. They spotted the suspect ahead of them, and Eli gave Delanie a quiet update.

The woman slipped in between two cabins. "You stay on the pavement," Eli said to Cody. "I'll circle around back. One of us will hopefully head her off at the pass." Eli headed off the street, cutting between cabins as well.

Cody sprinted down the street. He saw his dad coming from the other direction. Frank nodded, and Cody pointed to indicate she'd left the road.

Cody stopped a couple of cabins before the spot where he thought she'd turned off. He didn't want to give himself away by making too much noise.

Delanie's voice spoke through his earpiece. "Frankie apprehended the suspect in the act. He's bringing her out and will meet you on the street."

Another couple of seconds, and both Frankie and Eli came from between two cabins. Cody would swear the woman in cuffs was Lexi, but as he drew closer, the resemblance waned.

"Here's your girl," Frankie announced.

She wore a bored expression that roused Cody's anger. The sheriff showed up and read her the Miranda rights. Both the sheriff and Cody's dad stood in the background, letting Frankie and Eli handle the questioning.

"Who are you working for?" Eli demanded.

Everybody knew the answer, but they needed her to say it for the record.

She chomped on her gum and ignored them.

"Your choice," Frankie said. "We'll take you in and book you. We've got no problem charging you with arson. And whoever is calling the shots goes scot-free."

Cody saw a flash of fear in her eyes. Eli handed her off to the sheriff. "Take her in."

"Wait. What will happen if I tell you who I'm working for?"

"I'll ask the DA to go easy on you. Maybe lower your charge to a misdemeanor with a fine." The sheriff acted like he was doing her a big favor, but Cody knew that was all they could charge her with anyway. However, the fear of jail was loosening her lips.

"I'm an actress from LA. My agent hired me to play this part. He promised I wouldn't get into trouble. The fires were just to scare his girlfriend into going back to him."

Why does everyone keep referring to Lexi as Jamison Price's girlfriend?

"Tell us the exact agreement you made with Jamison, how much he's paying you, and how this acting job works," Frankie said, laying out all the information they needed from her.

"Jamison agreed to sign me with his agency if I could convince the neighbors I was Alexandria Eastridge."

She did have Lexi's build but wasn't nearly as graceful or pretty.

"He rented me a cabin and stocked it with food. I'm only allowed to leave when he calls me. I go where he sends me and do what he tells me. He promised if I could pull this off without getting caught, he'd get me a starring role. I've been trying to get my career off the ground for a long time." She started to cry. "He promised no one would get hurt." She sniffed.

"How could you believe that?" Cody felt certain no one could be that stupid.

"What are you supposed to do next?" Eli asked.

She sniffed. "Call and let him know someone saw me and that I started another fire."

"Why don't you go ahead with that now?" Cody suggested. "This one is for the Academy Award."

She pulled the cell phone off her belt and speed-dialed Jamison Price. "Hey, it's me." She used a different voice with him than she had with them—sexier, softer, blonder. "Done and done. Yes, sir." She closed the phone.

"Where do we go from here?" Cody asked. They had a lot of pieces, but the puzzle wasn't finished yet, at least not for him.

His dad glanced at the sheriff. "These are small fish, as far as I'm concerned. I'd like to see Jamison Price pay for this and what he does to young girls with the promise of fame attached. He's nothing but a user."

"So what are you thinking?" the young sheriff asked with his brow creased.

"I'd like a little time."

The sheriff nodded.

"Can you spare two men? We'll put these two suspects under twenty-four-hour guard. They can proceed with Mr. Price as if things are normal. I'll get in touch with the LA district attorney and see if he's willing to charge Price with anything."

"Yes, sir. We'll do whatever you need," replied the sheriff.

Cody watched with renewed respect as his dad turned over the two they'd arrested to the sheriff and his men. He covered all the details.

Then his dad said, "Let's head back to your place."

The four of them headed back to Cody's and then crossed the street to fill everyone in on the outcome all at once. "I think we need to celebrate!" Essie glowed with her excitement. "Let's have a barbecue, play games, and spend the day together."

Everyone responded with jovial agreements, but Cody was watching Lexi as she sat quietly in the corner of the room, her head bent down. She failed to share the exuberance of the rest of the group. He touched her arm and motioned with his head for her to follow. She did, and they slipped outside.

"I thought you'd be happy. The nightmare is over." He led the way across the street, and they sat on the steps leading to his front porch.

"I am happy, and sad, and a million other things. But mostly I'm angry. This guy manipulated me as an impressionable teen, and a dozen years later, he's still trying to manipulate my life."

"He refers to you as his girlfriend. Any reason he might still think you are?" There was a thread of jealousy in Cody's tone.

"No. I ended that long ago."

❧

Frank headed across the street. He looked like a man with something on his mind. "You have a few minutes?"

Lexi nodded.

"I'd like to speak to you about the case." He glanced at Cody, who rose from his spot next to her.

"You can stay. There is nothing about this you don't know

anyway." She smiled at Cody.

He sat back down, and Frank settled on the other side of her. "Would you be willing to testify against Jamison regarding his sexual advances and promises when you were a minor?"

Fear shot through her. If she did, her parents might disown her. But how many more girls would he hurt and take advantage of if she didn't?

She drew in a deep breath. "Yeah. Yeah, I would."

"Are there others who might be willing to follow your lead?"

Lexi thought. Rayanna came to mind. Then Tianna. And there was Claudette. "I think so." Lexi nodded. "I think I could convince a few of the girls he's hurt along the way to stand up and be heard."

"It could get ugly." Frank's expression was filled with compassion. His eyes reminded her of Cody's—dear, sweet, wonderful Cody.

Fear surged like adrenaline through her veins.

"He'll probably make this out to be your fault. Your reputation will be dragged through the mud. Any man you've ever had relations with might be brought in to testify, if the DA will even consider the case to begin with."

Lexi sighed and remembered the young girl sitting in the waiting room the last time she left Jamison's office. "I have to at least try. It's the right thing." With the decision made, peace settled over her. Maybe this would right some of the wrongs in her past.

But she knew in her heart only God could do that. Only He could take what was meant for evil and make it good. Only He could redeem the years the locusts had eaten. Only He could somehow cause these twelve years of sinful choices to work together for good. And in her heart was a ray of hope that He would.

Frank rose. "Then I'm going to make the call, if you're sure."

Lexi smiled, actually tasting freedom. "I've never been surer in my life."

Frank's eyes reflected his approval. He glanced at Cody. "I'll use your cabin and make the necessary calls. It's loud and festive across the street. You two ought to join in the celebration."

"We will." Lexi rose.

Frank disappeared behind Cody's front door. She glanced at Cody. He'd not said much. "You coming?"

He grabbed her hand and pulled her back down on the step next to him. "I just want you to know that I'll walk through this with you, if you'll let me."

His sincere chocolate eyes melted her heart. She had to be strong—more for his sake than hers. She chose her words with care. "I'd appreciate that. I'm sure I'll need some good friends in my corner. Heaven knows all my friends on the LA scene will probably never speak to me again."

When she used the word *friends*, a little of the hope left his face. "I'll be whatever you need me to be." His thumb caressed hers.

I need you to forget me and not gaze at me with such hurt and longing. "True friends are hard to come by in this world, and I know you'll always be there for me. Thank you. Now let's go party." She stood and pulled him up with her.

Frank came out on the porch. "Lexi, before you head across the street, I want you to put in a call to Jamison. I'd like to listen and record it if you don't mind."

Lexi dropped Cody's hand. "You can come if you want—and be my friend to lean on."

❧

Friend? If that's all you'll give me, then I'll take it.

Cody followed Lexi and his dad into his A-frame log home.

"Frankie brought some equipment down so I can record the conversation. We'll be able to hear both of you talking. Are you okay with that?" His dad glanced at him, and Cody knew he only wanted to spare him pain. And protect Lexi's privacy, of course.

Lexi nodded but glanced at Cody, too. Her eyes begged him not to hold whatever he heard against her.

"Lexi, I can meet you at your grandparents' whenever you are through."

She shook her head. "If you truly are going to walk with me through this mess, you'll hear all of it sooner or later—the good, the bad, and the ugly. It may as well start today."

While his dad got everything hooked up and ready, Lexi paced.

"Can I pray for you?" Cody asked.

"Would you? When I walked out of Jamison's office six weeks ago, I never planned to see or speak to him ever again. Having to, especially in light of his latest stunt, makes me feel physically ill."

"I understand. What you're doing is hard and courageous." His heart swelled with admiration for her. He clasped both of her hands in his. They trembled in his hold. "Lord, these next few months will be hard on Lexi. Will You show Yourself real to her? Fill her with Your power, Your peace, and Your wisdom. I ask all this in the mighty name of Your Son, amen."

She smiled. "Thank you." Their gazes connected, and neither pulled their hands apart.

Cody longed to say so much more but couldn't. Lexi had made the boundaries clear, and he'd respect them. Otherwise, he might lose even her friendship, and a little Lexi was better than none at all.

"You ready to get this show on the road?" Frank had just finished hooking up the last wire. He held Lexi's cell phone out toward her. "You've got to sound 100 percent believable—100 percent."

"Remember all those acting lessons you told me about?" Lexi cracked up, probably alleviating some of her tension. "I told you I was terrible."

Cody winked. "Today you won't be, because it matters." He knew she could do it.

She took her phone with a quivering hand. Taking a deep breath, she closed her eyes and exhaled slowly, deliberately.

She punched one number and put the phone to her ear. Jamison was apparently still on her speed dial. That fact bugged Cody, and he knew jealousy reared its ugly green head.

"Jamison Price Talent Agency. This is Evelyn. How may I direct your call?" She spoke into Lexi's ear but also over a speaker of some sort.

"This is Alexandria for Jamison." She glanced at Cody, and he gave her a thumbs-up. She paced as far as the wires permitted.

"Babe! I've been dying to hear from you. How are you? I've seen the news. Man, I've been worried sick."

I bet you have, you lying snake. Just hearing his voice brought a negative reaction to Cody.

"I've been thinking about you, too." Her words—sounding so sweet and sincere—brought an ache to Cody's heart. "I got your messages."

"Will you come home, baby? Home to your papa bear?" Lexi cringed in disgust, making Cody feel better.

"What exactly are you saying, Jamison?" Again her voice rang pleasant and true—not mirroring her expression at all.

"Baby, I miss you. I wanted to wait and say this in person, but I want you back—all the way back."

"What does that mean?"

"Fly home today, and I'll make sweet love to you all night long. Just the way it used to be. Just me and you, baby. Just me and you."

Cody had balled his hands into fists. How dare that guy?

Lexi sat down. "That's the thing, Jamison. It never was just me and you. You've slept with almost every woman you represent at one time or another."

"I know, but that's in the past. I've sown my wild oats, and I'm ready to be with you for the rest of my life. Fly home to Papa Bear."

"What about modeling?"

"No more, unless you want to. Of course, you can model for me anytime."

The implication made Cody's blood boil.

"I have, however, received a very lucrative offer with your name on the contract. Totally your call, though."

What a piece of work.

"Do you want me to have Evelyn call and book your flight home? I'll even pay."

"You must really want me back." Sarcasm laced itself through Lexi's tone. "You don't ever pay."

"I will from now on if that's what it takes to bring you back."

"I'll tell you what it will take. I need to hear exactly what is on your mind once I get there."

"Baby, you drive a hard bargain."

"I learned from the best," Lexi reminded him.

"Flattery will get you everywhere. I want to live with you and be with you every day from here on out."

"What about a ring?"

"Aw, baby, we've had that discussion. Come on, you know I'm not the marrying kind."

"I want the ring. I want your name. I want a family. And I don't want to model—not ever again. No matter how much money is involved." Lexi seemed to enjoy her newfound power. "Two carats, Jamison. With baguettes."

"Alexandria! You think you can call all the shots?"

"If you want me back, I can. And a prenup that says if you cheat on me, I get 50 percent of your assets."

"Baby, marriage is forever. Who needs a prenup?" His voice was syrupy sweet.

"My assets say I do."

"I'm lovesick. Whatever you want. Meet me in my office tomorrow afternoon, and I'll show you carats and baguettes."

Lexi squealed. "Jamison, you've made me the happiest woman on earth. See you tomorrow." And she closed her cell phone.

Cody wondered if the offer tempted her, and at the same time, he hated himself for doubting her. She'd said she once thought herself in love with Jamison. Now he offered all she'd once longed for. Was she really over him? He searched her face for the answer but found nothing.

"Well played, Lexi. Well played. Will he be surprised when you show up tomorrow with me and the LA DA in tow."

Lexi smiled, but a sadness resided in her eyes, only confirming Cody's fears. She was having second thoughts. She wanted what Jamison was offering. Cody had made the same offer, but she wasn't interested. After all the snake had done to her, she still loved him. How or why, Cody couldn't for the life of him fathom.

fifteen

Lexi hung up the phone feeling nauseated. She closed her eyes and tried to regain her equilibrium. Thank heaven her feeling for that man died years ago. All she wanted was to see him pay for all he'd done to her and others like her.

When she reopened her eyes, Cody studied her. He wore a hurt expression.

"I'm sorry you had to hear some of that. I'm going across the street to hold baby Camden."

"I'll stay behind and help my dad pack all this up." Frank had already begun dismantling the high-tech communications center he'd set up last night.

"I'll see you in a while then."

Lexi couldn't wait to hold the little guy. There was something so pure and precious about a baby; it was easy to forget her own problems. They just kind of rocked away.

⁂

When Lexi shut the door, Cody's dad stopped unhooking wires and looked directly into Cody's eyes. "You all right, son?"

Cody blew out a long, slow breath. "Partially. It was hard to hear."

"Because you love her?" His dad raised one brow.

"That and I can't help but wonder how she's feeling about him."

"Ask her."

Part of him feared her answer. "If he does love her and

married her, it would right some of his wrongs."

"I don't think so. Your emotions are too close to reason through this. I believe anything she felt for him died many moons ago."

Cody wanted to hope, but doubt flew at him from all directions.

"I was wondering if you'd travel with us to LA. I know you took this week off, and I thought Lexi might need you for moral support. You two seem to have grown close."

"Yeah, I'll go, but I may need you for moral support before all is said and done."

"I'll be there for you."

"Would it bother you or Mom if I did marry a girl like Lexi?"

His dad put the last piece of equipment into the trunk and shut it. "A girl with a past?"

"Yeah."

"Not as long as her future was secure in Christ."

"Grace?"

"Grace. How can we offer less?"

Cody's respect for his dad moved up a notch, and it was already at the top of the chart. He hugged him. "Thanks, Dad. I'll see you over at the Newcomb's."

When Cody walked in, the first thing to catch his eye was Camden snuggled in Lexi's arms. She was alone in the living room in the same rocker her grandmother had rocked her in as a baby. And wafting through the air was a sweet rendition of "Softly and Tenderly Jesus Is Calling" "Come home, come home, ye who are weary, come home; earnestly, tenderly, Jesus is calling, calling, O sinner, come home!" Even from the front door, Cody didn't miss the tear that trickled down Lexi's cheek.

Cody's heart longed to go to her, but he didn't. He joined everyone else in the family room, but he would never forget the sight of her with his nephew. He yearned for things with Lexi that would never be.

&

Having Cody along for the trip to LA was bittersweet for Lexi. She hated him seeing how low she'd once fallen, but maybe it was a good reminder for him of how unsuitable they were for each other.

They boarded the elevator, all riding together to the tenth floor. Cody, Frank, and Mr. Martinez, the man from the district attorney's office, were all going to wait in the hall until Lexi gained access to Jamison's office.

"Good afternoon, Evelyn." Lexi marched right past the receptionist to Jamison's office door.

"Wait. I should announce you."

"He's expecting me." She breezed right through the door, half expecting to find him with another girl.

But he was alone, perched behind his desk, his eyes on his computer screen. "Jamison, darling. I'm home." She slipped her purse off her shoulder, and as she did, she punched nine on her cell phone, which would ring Cody in the hall, letting them know she was inside.

Jamison jumped up and came around the desk, sweeping her into his arms. The kiss he laid on her made her want to puke, but she didn't want to arouse his suspicions, so she allowed him to dip her back and lay one on her. Not the position she'd planned to be in when the three men burst through his door, badges out.

"Jamison Price, we are here to question you regarding statutory rape."

At Frank's words, Jamison nearly let her fall on her head.

She grabbed hold of his arm and pulled herself upright.

Lexi stepped away from him as Mr. Martinez listed the witnesses. He'd already found two other women—besides her—to testify of his escapades with minors.

He glared at Lexi. "You did this. This is your fault."

Cody stepped between them. "You have no one to blame but yourself. And you deserve whatever happens to you. If you end up in prison, they hate child molesters. You'll get what you deserve."

Cody ushered Lexi out of the office. Two men wearing LAPD uniforms questioned Evelyn. When they climbed into the elevator, Lexi fell apart. Cody pulled her into his arms, kissing the top of her head and whispering words she couldn't hear over her own sobs. The emotion that hit Lexi blindsided her. It was over—all of it. The fires, the ordeal with Jamison, Cody. Today all things good and bad ended.

She longed to wrap her arms around Cody's neck and kiss him long and hard. But love gave more than it took, so today she officially laid down any claim she might have on Cody's heart. This was good-bye, and someday he'd thank her when he found a really nice girl to settle down with.

He led her down the street to the Starbucks. They'd planned to wait there for the other two. This was her chance to say good-bye before Frank and Mr. Martinez met up with them.

Once inside Starbucks, Lexi went in the restroom and wiped her makeup-blotched face with a wet paper towel. When she came out, Cody sat at a table for two with a couple of Java Chip Frappuccinos beckoning her.

He constantly touched her in ways she never expected—thoughtful, sweet ways. No matter where life took her, she knew for certain she'd never forget Cody Cooper.

"You told me this was your favorite afternoon pick-me-up."

She smiled. "And you remembered. I'm impressed."

Cody swallowed, and she watched his Adam's apple rise and fall. "There isn't much about you that I'll ever forget."

Lexi laughed, fighting the urge to turn to mush. "Until the next pretty girl comes along. Then I'll be old news, and you'll replace my info with hers."

"Not likely. Did you know I fell in love with you long before I met you?"

The news surprised her. "And then you encountered the real me at the airport. The shrew. Bet you wished then that you'd run far and fast."

"I wouldn't have missed knowing you for anything." Sincere but sad brown eyes caught her gaze.

You're killing me here. "Are you trying to make me cry?"

He tipped his head to one side in his endearing way. "Nope. Just trying to keep from it myself."

"Cody." Her tone grew serious. "I'm glad I didn't miss you, either. And I'm sure I'll see you again sometime when I visit my grandparents."

He gave her hand a squeeze. "You're not going back with us?"

She shook her head.

"I sort of figured."

His dad and Mr. Martinez entered the shop.

"I'm heading out." Mr. Martinez shook Frank's hand and then Cody's. "I've got your number and will be in touch," he said to her. "I'll need to do an in-depth interview. Not sure how far this will go, but we're willing to give it a shot."

Lexi toyed with her straw. "I'll be around whenever you need me."

The assistant district attorney nodded. "Good-bye, all." He carried his briefcase out the door and was gone.

"How did things go after we left?" Lexi asked Frank.

"Let's just say Jamison Price was not a happy camper."

"Thank you for believing in me and for everything you did."

Frank nodded. "It was my pleasure." He glanced at Cody. "Our pleasure."

"What time is your flight?" Lexi pushed her hair behind one ear.

Frank checked his watch. "We have several hours. Can we see you home?"

"I'll grab a cab. I live a long way from here." Lexi rose.

"Guess this is good-bye then." Frank glanced from Cody to Lexi. Then he stood and hugged her. "Building your future on a lie isn't the best way to start afresh," he whispered in her ear.

He turned to Cody. "I'll meet you at the car. Take your time. We're in no hurry." With that he turned and was gone.

Lexi sat back down.

"Sorry. My family isn't known for being subtle."

Lexi giggled. "Your family's great."

Cody stood. "There is no reason to drag this out."

"No, there isn't." She stood as well.

The moment was awkward. She didn't look into his eyes. Couldn't. "Cody." She swallowed. "Would you kiss me?"

A puzzled expression settled on his face. "Sure." He leaned down and planted a kiss on her cheek.

"That wasn't exactly what I had in mind. I was hoping to erase Jamison's kiss with yours."

⁂

Cody's heart thudded a steady rhythm. "You want me to kiss you?"

She nodded. "If you don't mind."

Mind? No, he surely didn't mind. "I guess if I have to," he teased.

"You probably think this is stupid, but it may be years before I get kissed, and I don't want Jamison's lips from this afternoon lingering on mine for who knows how long."

"I thought you still had feelings for the guy." Cody admitted his misgivings.

"Oh, I do—"

His heart dropped after just shooting for the moon.

"Loathing, anger, distrust."

Cody placed his hands on her waist. "The proposal never tempted you?"

"Are you kidding? Not for a second. He is a liar and a loser."

He drew his brows together, certain he'd never figure out God's fairer sex. "Then why the tears?"

"You thought I was pining away for Jamison?" She laughed. "Not on your life." Then she grew serious and stopped looking everywhere but at him.

"I'll miss you and my grandparents. It's been a tumultuous few weeks. But my feelings for Jamison died many years ago."

He moved his hands to the side of her face. "I'll miss you, too, and if things ever change for you, I'll probably still be waiting."

Determined to make the most of this last chance to woo her, he moved slowly toward her, looking deep into her eyes. When their lips met, emotions exploded inside Cody. He took his time, filling the kiss with all the love and tenderness he could muster. When he finally raised his head, she wore a dazed expression. She released a soft, contented sigh.

"Was that your best shot?" He saw the mirth in her eyes.

" 'Fraid so. But I'll try again if you like."

She touched her lips. "No need. Jamison's kiss is gone, and the memory of your kiss will live on." She traced his jaw.

"I hate good-byes, so I'm going to the restroom. Will you do me a favor and be gone when I come out?"

He nodded and pulled her into one last hug. "Bye, Lexi." He stumbled over the words. Then he turned her loose and walked away, praying all the while. *God, bring her back somehow.*

❧

With tears in her eyes, Lexi watched Cody walk away, and unbeknownst to him, he carried her heart in his hand. Was she making the biggest mistake of her life? How many days did it take a broken heart to heal? And how long would it hurt to simply breathe?

Lexi sat back down at the table and stared out the window. Feeling lost, she wondered where to go from here. With no desire to stay in LA, where could she go? Even after all she'd been through, her heart still longed to return to the mountains and the most beautiful lake in the world.

Frank said Mr. Martinez would make certain that Jamison Price made a very public apology for all he'd done to slander her name. He hoped it would air on the ten o'clock news tonight. What a good man Frank Cooper was, and Cody was his father's son. The Coopers weren't perfect, but they were the closest to Christlike she'd ever seen, except for Gram and Gramps.

She needed to call Gram to tell her she'd have a courier pick up her things. She should have brought them but took the coward's way out for two reasons. She didn't want to have to mess with luggage while they were dealing with Jamison, and she didn't want to see Gram's face when she discovered Lexi wasn't coming back this evening. But now, in a matter of hours, Gram would know anyway.

She opened her purse to fish out her cell phone. Her little

Bible caught her eye, and she pulled it out as well. Gram had given it to her just last week. She unsnapped the cover and flipped through the pages. It smelled new and fresh—the pages pristine and crisp, the gold edges still shiny and new.

A new creature in Christ. That was her. Like the pages of this Bible, she was whiter than snow. The epiphany astounded her. She'd been forgiven and stood before God and the whole world new, clean, and restored to her Father. His grace had been poured into her life. She could see it in the way this whole thing worked out.

A sermon she'd heard recently echoed through her head. She could either live in the forgiveness, live the life of the new creature, or she could remain stuck in the condemnation of her past. Which would she choose? She ran her fingertips over the cover of her Bible. She raised it to her face and smelled the new leather. Then she hugged it against her heart. Which would it be—free and new or stuck in her past?

❧

"I'm sorry, son. I know you're hurting." Cody's dad slapped his back a couple of times as they went through the tunnel between the airport and the plane to board their flight back to Reno.

"Time heals all wounds, or so they say," Cody said. He found their row in the plane and settled into the window seat. His dad took the aisle seat. The plane wasn't full, so they didn't have a middle passenger.

"Do you think Lexi will ever accept God's forgiveness and forgive herself?" Cody asked once he'd buckled his seat belt.

"She might. The whole Cooper clan is praying for her. Does she stand a chance?"

Cody chuckled. "I hope not, but she may never choose me, even if God gets through."

The aisle was filled with passengers as they stowed their things in the overhead bins.

"No, she may not. She told me once that she couldn't make plans until tomorrow."

"What does that even mean?" Cody's frustration came out with his words.

"I asked the same thing, and she explained that her life was on hold until the whole fire thing was cleared up and she'd been exonerated. In other words, until tomorrow came and she was free, she couldn't move forward."

"Well then today is tomorrow, and she chose not to move forward with me."

His dad nodded.

Cody closed his eyes and leaned his head against the side of the plane. *Tomorrow is here. And it will be followed by many more lonely tomorrows.* Days of missing Lexi. Nights of wishing she'd included him in her tomorrows. *Lord, it looks like it will be just You and me for a while longer. Help me get over Lexi and move on to the future You have planned for me.*

"Is this seat taken?"

Her voice penetrated his prayer. Was it his imagination? Did he dare open his eyes, lest he face more disappointment?

"Lexi, you're joining us?" His dad's voice carried enough excitement for both of them.

When he glanced over, his dad climbed out of his seat to allow Lexi to pass through. She shined her biggest smile on him, and Cody sat up straighter.

"Hi." He wasn't sure what to say, and he didn't want to go getting any ideas, so he let her take the lead.

"Hi." She buckled her seat belt, and his dad settled back into his place on the aisle. He wore a face-splitting grin. He obviously believed what Cody dared not hope.

When Cody couldn't stand the suspense another minute, he asked, "Where are you headed?"

"Home." She turned to face him. Something was different. The shadows were gone from her eyes. "I'm going home to stay."

Cody swallowed. His eyes searched her face. She smiled and placed her hand in his.

His pulse increased, and a seed of hope sprouted in his heart.

"I love you, Cody."

It was the first time she'd said those precious words, and he'd not expected them, making the sound twice as sweet.

"You do?" He couldn't hide his surprise. *Lord, this is better than I even imagined.* "You love me?" Sheer joy danced out with the words. "You really love me?"

She nodded and laughed. "Really."

"Dad, she loves me! Lexi loves me." And he loved saying the words. Each time drove the truth home in his mind.

"I know, son. I heard. Now why don't you kiss her already?"

Cody obeyed his dad's suggestion, leaning across her seat and kissing her with awe at this blessing.

"I can't believe you love me," he whispered, her face mere inches from his.

Her expression grew serious. "With all my heart." She laid her hand on his chest. "I'm giving you my very grateful heart, and I'm asking you to treasure it—today, tomorrow, and always."

A promise that would be easy to make and easy to keep.

epilogue

Cody stood on the observation deck, halfway to the top of Heavenly. His dad, Brady, Frankie, Eli, and Alph stood nearby. For Cody, today truly was heavenly. He and Lexi would vow their tomorrows to each other before his immediate family and her grandparents on this cold, snowy, Christmasy day. Her parents were out of the country and unable to attend.

Lexi's favorite verse was Psalm 51:7, "Cleanse me with hyssop, and I will be clean; wash me, and I will be whiter than snow." So today was an appropriate day for them to wed. The snow would be a constant reminder that she was clean before God, forgiven, free to move into a pure relationship with Cody.

The women made their way out onto the cold deck—all of them but Lexi. Alph went and met her in the small gift shop where she waited. Sunni turned on an iPod, and the wedding march blared out. Lexi came into view, beautiful on her grandfather's arm. Cody had convinced her to wear white, another remembrance of her righteous standing before God because of her relationship with Jesus Christ.

Lexi didn't wear a veil, and her face glowed. Their eyes connected. His heart pounded like an Indian drum during a war dance. When she reached him, he took her hands in his. They faced each other, and tears glistened in her eyes. The snow glistened beyond, covering the earth in a blanket of white.

Cody had never been more grateful for grace than at that moment. Grace that Lexi had accepted. Grace that brought them together. Grace that would fill each tomorrow.

A Letter To Our Readers

Dear Reader:
In order that we might better contribute to your reading enjoyment, we would appreciate your taking a few minutes to respond to the following questions. We welcome your comments and read each form and letter we receive. When completed, please return to the following:

Fiction Editor
Heartsong Presents
PO Box 719
Uhrichsville, Ohio 44683

1. Did you enjoy reading *Until Tomorrow* by Jeri Odell?
   ❏ Very much! I would like to see more books by this author!
   ❏ Moderately. I would have enjoyed it more if

   _____
   _____
   _____

2. Are you a member of **Heartsong Presents**? ❏ Yes ❏ No
   If no, where did you purchase this book? _____
   _____

3. How would you rate, on a scale from 1 (poor) to 5 (superior), the cover design? _____

4. On a scale from 1 (poor) to 10 (superior), please rate the following elements.

   ____ Heroine   ____ Plot
   ____ Hero   ____ Inspirational theme
   ____ Setting   ____ Secondary characters

5. These characters were special because? _____

_____

_____

6. How has this book inspired your life? _____

_____

_____

7. What settings would you like to see covered in future
   Heartsong Presents books? _____

_____

_____

8. What are some inspirational themes you would like to see
   treated in future books? _____

_____

_____

9. Would you be interested in reading other **Heartsong
   Presents** titles? ❏ Yes ❏ No

10. Please check your age range:
    ❏ Under 18   ❏ 18-24
    ❏ 25-34   ❏ 35-45
    ❏ 46-55   ❏ Over 55

Name _____

Occupation _____

Address _____

City, State, Zip_____

Vermont WEDDINGS

3 stories in 1

Three romances overcome challenges in small-town Goosebury by Pamela Griffin. Three women from Goosebury, Vermont, are treading carefully when it comes to finding love.

Contemporary, paperback, 352 pages, 5³/₁₆" x 8"

Heartng

CONTEMPORARY ROMANCE IS CHEAPER BY THE DOZEN!

Any 12 Heartsong Presents titles for only $27.00*

Buy any assortment of twelve *Heartsong Presents* titles and save 25% off the already discounted price of $2.97 each!

*plus $4.00 shipping and handling per order and sales tax where applicable. If outside the U.S. please call 740-922-7280 for shipping charges.

HEARTSONG PRESENTS TITLES AVAILABLE NOW:

____HP561 *Ton's Vow*, K. Cornelius
____HP562 *Family Ties*, J. L. Barton
____HP565 *An Unbreakable Hope*, K. Billerbeck
____HP566 *The Baby Quilt*, J. Livingston
____HP569 *Ageless Love*, L. Bliss
____HP570 *Beguiling Masquerade*, C. G. Page
____HP573 *In a Land Far Far Away*, M. Panagiotopoulos
____HP574 *Lambert's Pride*, L. A. Coleman and R. Hauck
____HP577 *Anita's Fortune*, K. Cornelius
____HP578 *The Birthday Wish*, J. Livingston
____HP581 *Love Online*, K. Billerbeck
____HP582 *The Long Ride Home*, A. Boeshaar
____HP585 *Compassion's Charm*, D. Mills
____HP586 *A Single Rose*, P. Griffin
____HP589 *Changing Seasons*, C. Reece and J. Reece-Demarco
____HP590 *Secret Admirer*, G. Sattler
____HP593 *Angel Incognito*, J. Thompson
____HP594 *Out on a Limb*, G. Gaymer Martin
____HP597 *Let My Heart Go*, B. Huston
____HP598 *More Than Friends*, T. H. Murray
____HP601 *Timing is Everything*, T. V. Bateman
____HP602 *Dandelion Bride*, J. Livingston
____HP605 *Picture Imperfect*, N. J. Farrier
____HP606 *Mary's Choice*, Kay Cornelius
____HP609 *Through the Fire*, C. Lynxwiler
____HP613 *Chorus of One*, J. Thompson
____HP614 *Forever in My Heart*, L. Ford
____HP617 *Run Fast, My Love*, P. Griffin
____HP618 *One Last Christmas*, J. Livingston
____HP621 *Forever Friends*, T. H. Murray
____HP622 *Time Will Tell*, L. Bliss
____HP625 *Love's Image*, D. Mayne
____HP626 *Down From the Cross*, J. Livingston
____HP629 *Look to the Heart*, T. Fowler
____HP630 *The Flat Marriage Fix*, K. Hayse
____HP633 *Longing for Home*, C. Lynxwiler

____HP634 *The Child Is Mine*, M. Colvin
____HP637 *Mother's Day*, J. Livingston
____HP638 *Real Treasure*, T. Davis
____HP641 *The Pastor's Assignment*, K. O'Brien
____HP642 *What's Cooking*, G. Sattler
____HP645 *The Hunt for Home*, G. Aiken
____HP649 *4th of July*, J. Livingston
____HP650 *Romanian Rhapsody*, D. Franklin
____HP653 *Lakeside*, M. Davis
____HP654 *Alaska Summer*, M. H. Flinkman
____HP657 *Love Worth Finding*, C. M. Hake
____HP658 *Love Worth Keeping*, J. Livingston
____HP661 *Lambert's Code*, R. Hauck
____HP665 *Bah Humbug, Mrs. Scrooge*, J. Livingston
____HP666 *Sweet Charity*, J. Thompson
____HP669 *The Island*, M. Davis
____HP670 *Miss Menace*, N. Lavo
____HP673 *Flash Flood*, D. Mills
____HP677 *Banking on Love*, J. Thompson
____HP678 *Lambert's Peace*, R. Hauck
____HP681 *The Wish*, L. Bliss
____HP682 *The Grand Hotel*, M. Davis
____HP685 *Thunder Bay*, B. Loughner
____HP686 *Always a Bridesmaid*, A. Boeshaar
____HP689 *Unforgettable*, J. L. Barton
____HP690 *Heritage*, M. Davis
____HP693 *Dear John*, K. V. Sawyer
____HP694 *Riches of the Heart*, T. Davis
____HP697 *Dear Granny*, P. Griffin
____HP698 *With a Mother's Heart*, J. Livingston
____HP701 *Cry of My Heart*, L. Ford
____HP702 *Never Say Never*, L. N. Dooley
____HP705 *Listening to Her Heart*, J. Livingston
____HP706 *The Dwelling Place*, K. Miller
____HP709 *That Wilder Boy*, K. V. Sawyer
____HP710 *To Love Again*, J. L. Barton
____HP713 *Secondhand Heart*, J. Livingston
____HP714 *Anna's Journey*, N. Toback

(If ordering from this page, please remember to include it with the order form.)

Presents

___HP717 *Merely Players*, K. Kovach
___HP718 *In His Will*, C. Hake
___HP721 *Through His Grace*, K. Hake
___HP722 *Christmas Mommy*, T. Fowler
___HP725 *By His Hand*, J. Johnson
___HP726 *Promising Angela*, K. V. Sawyer
___HP729 *Bay Hideaway*, B. Loughner
___HP730 *With Open Arms*, J. L. Barton
___HP733 *Safe in His Arms*, T. Davis
___HP734 *Larkspur Dreams*, A. Higman and
          J. A. Thompson
___HP737 *Darcy's Inheritance*, L. Ford
___HP738 *Picket Fence Pursuit*, J. Johnson
___HP741 *The Heart of the Matter*, K. Dykes
___HP742 *Prescription for Love*, A. Boeshaar
___HP745 *Family Reunion*, J. L. Barton
___HP746 *By Love Acquitted*, Y. Lehman
___HP749 *Love by the Yard*, G. Sattler
___HP750 *Except for Grace*, T. Fowler
___HP753 *Long Trail to Love*, P. Griffin
___HP754 *Red Like Crimson*, J. Thompson
___HP757 *Everlasting Love*, L. Ford
___HP758 *Wedded Bliss*, K. Y'Barbo
___HP761 *Double Blessing*, D. Mayne
___HP762 *Photo Op*, L. A. Coleman
___HP765 *Sweet Sugared Love*, P. Griffin
___HP766 *Pursuing the Goal*, J. Johnson
___HP769 *Who Am I?*, L. N. Dooley

___HP770 *And Baby Makes Five*, G. G. Martin
___HP773 *A Matter of Trust*, L. Harris
___HP774 *The Groom Wore Spurs*, J. Livingston
___HP777 *Seasons of Love*, E. Goddard
___HP778 *The Love Song*, J. Thompson
___HP781 *Always Yesterday*, J. Odell
___HP782 *Trespassed Hearts*, L. A. Coleman
___HP785 *If the Dress Fits*, D. Mayne
___HP786 *White as Snow*, J. Thompson
___HP789 *The Bride Wore Coveralls*, D. Ullrick
___HP790 *Garlic and Roses*, G. Martin
___HP793 *Coming Home*, T. Fowler
___HP794 *John's Quest*, C. Dowdy
___HP797 *Building Dreams*, K. Y'Barbo
___HP798 *Courting Disaster*, A. Boeshaar
___HP801 *Picture This*, N. Farrier
___HP802 *In Pursuit of Peace*, J. Johnson
___HP805 *Only Today*, J. Odell
___HP806 *Out of the Blue*, J. Thompson
___HP809 *Suited for Love*, L.A. Coleman
___HP810 *Butterfly Trees*, G. Martin
___HP813 *Castles in the Air*, A. Higman and
          J. A. Thompson
___HP814 *The Preacher Wore a Gun*, J. Livingston
___HP817 *By the Beckoning Sea*, C. G. Page
___HP818 *Buffalo Gal*, M. Connealy
___HP821 *Clueless Cowboy*, M. Connealy
___HP822 *Walk with Me*, B. Melby and C. Wienke

Great Inspirational Romance at a Great Price!

Heartsong Presents books are inspirational romances in
contemporary and historical settings, designed to give you an
enjoyable, spirit-lifting reading experience. You can choose
wonderfully written titles from some of today's best authors like
Wanda E. Brunstetter, Mary Connealy, Susan Page Davis,
Cathy Marie Hake, Joyce Livingston, and many others.

When ordering quantities less than twelve, above titles are $2.97 each.
Not all titles may be available at time of order.